ISBN 978-1-331-15408-2
PIBN 10151415

This book is a reproduction of an important historical work. Forgotten Books uses
state-of-the-art technology to digitally reconstruct the work, preserving the original format
whilst repairing imperfections present in the aged copy. In rare cases, an imperfection in
the original, such as a blemish or missing page, may be replicated in our edition. We do,
however, repair the vast majority of imperfections successfully; any imperfections that
remain are intentionally left to preserve the state of such historical works.

For support please visit www.forgottenbooks.com

English
Français
Deutsche
Italiano
Español
Português

www.forgottenbooks.com

Mythology Photography **Fiction**
Fishing Christianity **Art** Cooking
Essays Buddhism Freemasonry
Medicine **Biology** Music **Ancient
Egypt** Evolution Carpentry Physics
Dance Geology **Mathematics** Fitness
Shakespeare **Folklore** Yoga Marketing
Confidence Immortality Biographies
Poetry **Psychology** Witchcraft
Electronics Chemistry History **Law**
Accounting **Philosophy** Anthropology
Alchemy Drama Quantum Mechanics
Atheism Sexual Health **Ancient History**
Entrepreneurship Languages Sport
Paleontology Needlework Islam
Metaphysics Investment Archaeology
Parenting Statistics Criminology
Motivational

JACK GORDON,
KNIGHT ERRANT,
GOTHAM,
1883.

BY

W. C. HUDSON (Barclay North),

AUTHOR OF "THE DIAMOND BUTTON: WHOSE WAS IT?" ETC.

———

CASSELL PUBLISHING COMPANY

104 & 106 FOURTH AVENUE, NEW YORK

CONTENTS.

JÀCK GORDON, KNIGHT ERRANT, GOTHAM, 1883.

CHAPTER I.

AN AMATEUR CABMAN.

THERE are nights in the latter part of November in New York, when existence is a joy and exercise a delight ; when the weather is clear, cold and crisp ; when people walk briskly and set their feet down firmly ; when cheeks tingle from contact with the air yet suffer no discomfort ; when the gas shines through the plate-glass with increased brightness and the electric lights extend the area of their brilliancy—nights when the true son of Gotham would contemplate with contempt an offer to barter a walk from Twenty-third to Thirty-third street, for a stroll over the most famous promenade the world knows.

On such a night in 1883, a young man, about twenty-five or six, flung open the swinging doors of one of the hotels facing Madison Square, with unnecessary vigor, and stepped out on the pavement.

He was clad in irreproachable evening dress. The chill air suggested the wisdom of buttoning the heavy top-coat he wore. So he stopped to do so, and thus gave the cabmen, attentive upon him, a moment's suspense, while he considered which way he should go.

He disappointed them all by walking up Broadway. He was unmistakably a young man of fashion, his air showed that ; he was an athlete, his free carriage and elastic bearing determined that.

Spurning the attractions a famous restaurant held out on one side, and a hotel, which is, and was then, a popular rendezvous on the other, he continued on his way for several blocks, when he crossed to another hotel, under the portico of which stood a group of several young men, like himself irreproachably clad in evening dress.

As he approached, one of this group observed him and cried out, " Here's Jack Gordon ! Ask him. He knows all the women in town."

"What's up, ' Dizzy,' that you herald my approach with such vociferous and gratuitous information," asked the new-comer, inserting a single glass in his eye to look upon his friend and dropping it because it obscured his vision.

For answer he was led around the corner, and in front of a large window of the restaurant of the hotel from which the curtains were drawn. Here, seated some distance from the window, but in full view, sat a young and striking-looking woman, richly clad. On the opposite side of the table was a plainly dressed woman, the senior of the other by a dozen years, and quite evidently a servant.

" Well ? " said Gordon, inquiringly.

" What actress is that ? "

" Why do you think she is an actress ? " asked he in reply, again inserting his single glass and again dropping it immediately.

"Why ? Well, because she is so striking in appearance."

" A compliment to the fair damsels of the stage," interrupted Gordon.

" And because she is here in a restaurant at this

time of the night alone, accompanied only by a maid."

" Arguing thereby the possession of an acute observation upon your part," he commented.

" Well, who is she ? "

" The reliance you place upon my general information is touching. However, it is misplaced. I don't know who she is. But I am willing to bet she is not an actress with any one."

" Why ? "

" Because she is too conscious of the attention she is attracting from those in the room, and moreover embarrassed by it. Take my word for it, she is a private lady not accustomed to be on public exhibition."

" Well if she is not an actress, who is she ? "

" Again that inexhaustible reservoir—my information—fails to respond to drafts upon it. I don't know. I never saw her before. But why all this interest ? What has she done ? "

" Nothing, except to drive here in a hired cab," said one who had not yet spoken. " We were all standing here when she drove up, and started a discussion as to who and what she was."

" The town is sadly dull when you are driven to such desperate straits for amusement," said Gordon.

" ' Dizzy ' is trying to screw his courage up to speak to the fair unknown," said another, " but it slips down before he can force it up to the sticking-place."

" Bet you a bottle, not one of you dare do it," cried the one called ' Dizzy,' a blonde youth with pink cheeks, much undersized.

" There's a chance, Jack," said another. " I'm stumped. I don't dare do it."

" Oh, that's an easy bet—and too easily won," replied Gordon. " True, you may have to explain the little affair afterward at the station-house, but you could win your bet just the same. But, 'Dizzy,' I'll bet you a half-dozen I drive the lady home."

"Oh, oh, oh!" cried several voices.

"Drive her away from this restaurant—?"

"Drive her away from this restaurant. Do you think I'm a policeman? No, I'll drive away with her."

"That's what I mean. You will drive away from this restaurant with her, to her home?"

"Yes."

"Oh, come, that's a little too much. I know your audacity, but—"

"Do you refuse the bet?"

"Refuse it? No, if you insist upon it. It will do you good to have to pay for your bluffing once in a while."

"I'm not bluffing."

"You say you don't know her."

"I said so, and it's the truth. I never saw her before."

"All right, I'll take the bet. The wine to be opened here to-night."

"Very well. I shall insist that every one shall go out of sight except the one 'Dizzy' chooses to see that I carry out the bet."

"All right. I'll choose Will Robb."

"I'm satisfied," said Gordon. "Now please all go except Robb; I see that the fair lady is preparing to pay her bill."

The young men all hurried away, so as not to spoil the sport.

Gordon, closely followed by Robb, walked down the street a short distance to where a number of cabmen were standing.

"Where's Herrick?" he asked.

"Here I am, sor," said a liveried driver, coming from behind his cab; seeing who it was, he added

with a grin of recognition, " How are ye this ev'-
nin,' sor ? "

" I want your rig, Herrick."

" To drive it, sor."

" Yes. On the old terms. Double fare, and I
pay all damage."

" All right, sor," replied the cabman, with a
pleased grin ; " but it's the rattlin' jintlemin that
ye are."

" Never mind what I am, Herrick, but hurry up
with the livery and get the horse stripped," said
Gordon, taking off his top-coat.

Herrick opened the door and took from the box
under the seat a livery coat, and gave it to Jack, who
quickly donned it. Jack's coat was put in the box
with his crush hat, and a silk hat with a broad band
given him in exchange.

Robb, who was watching with amazement the
transformation of the stylish young man of fashion
into a dashing cabman, finally comprehended Jack's
purpose.

" It's a great lark, Jack," he said laughingly,
" but an awful roast on ' Dizzy '."

" Oh no, it's not," replied Gordon. " I bet him
I would drive the lady home. I did not say I would
ride with her as a companion. Besides, there is a
risk. I've got to secure her for a fare or I will
lose the bet."

" Oh, I don't object. I shall content myself with
reporting the fact."

" All right. You must follow in another cab."

" Certainly. But be lively, the woman is moving."

Gordon mounted the box, and taking the reins
drove up immediately in front of the restaurant
door.

Herrick, aided by the conversation, divined
Jack's purpose, and assisted him by soliciting the
lady as she issued from the hotel,

A cab was what the lady wanted and she entered it. The maid was about to follow her, when her mistress said :

" You go home by the street-car, Ellen. I will be there as soon as you. Wait for me at the door."

Then to Herrick she said :

" Fifty-fourth street."

" Fifty-fourth street and Broadway," called out Herrick to his substitute as he slammed the door. Gordon touched the horse smartly and drove off-at a rattling pace, Robb closely following in another cab.

As they turned into Broadway the young men were standing on the sidewalk awaiting developments. One caught a glimpse of the lady.

" There goes the woman now," he cried, " but I do not see Jack."

A moment later Robb passed, and was seen making excited gesticulations from the window and pointing to the preceding cab.

" And there's Robb following," cried another.

" Then Jack must be in the first one," said the one who had spoken. " ' Dizzy,' go in and order a half-dozen on ice."

" He's got the gall of a telegraph company," was ' Dizzy's ' only reply.

In the mean time Gordon drove rapidly up Broadway until nearly opposite a well-known theater, when he felt the check-strap vigorously pulled, and bending down to receive his order, he found his fare was endeavoring to attract the attention of a man on the sidewalk who was in the act of parting from another.

He drove close to the curbstone and assisted his fare in calling the man wanted, who responded by lifting his hat in a polite, though pronounced, manner, even with a flourish, and went to the cab window.

"I have been searching everywhere for you since I received your note," said the lady.

"I did not expect that," he replied coldly.

"Won't you get in?" she asked. "I want to talk to you."

"No ; it's useless," he replied. "There is nothing to talk about. You have my *ultimatum*."

This was said in so loud a tone that Gordon could not avoid hearing, and he was astonished both at the tone and manner.

After a moment's silence, the lady leaned forward and said :

"You know it is impossible—wholly impossible. Where am I to get what you demand? I have told you how I am circumstanced."

"That is not my lookout."

"Have you no mercy?"

"None whatever," said the man, without a change from his cold though courteous manner.

"I implore you," continued the lady, "not to push me to extremes—to have mercy upon me— to give me longer time. I have told you what I could and would do. The amount is greater in the end, if it is longer in payment."

"No, I must have the amount in one sum."

"I tell you it is simply impossible for me to obtain it. You make demands beyond my ability to comply. You know it well. What can you gain by driving me to ruin? If you expose me, not only will you not obtain the sum you demand, but you will have closed forever a very considerable source of income to you. As for this amount you might as well ask of me the wealth of the Vanderbilts."

"You wear on your person to-night three times the value of the sum I want."

"You ask me to commit a robbery. You know the jewels are not mine."

"Bah! you can pledge them and conveniently lose them until you can conveniently find them again."

"You are heartless. Don't go too far. You may lose all."

"I told you it was useless to talk. It is the same thing over again. Now then, Lucy, for the last time I say to you, if you do not produce the amount I demand, forthwith goes the package to Dr. Sherman. I'll give you until—to-day is Tuesday—I'll give you until Thursday night to comply with my demand; if you fail, then on Friday morning the package shall be in his hands."

"I beg—I entreat—I—"

"Now please stop that. I'll not have another word with you on the subject."

He stepped back to show that on his part the interview was ended.

The lady leaned so far forward that her head was entirely out of the window, and she spoke in tones of intense passion:

"You have gone too far, Cyril Renfrew. I will not give you one penny more. Do your worst. It means ruin to me, but death to you. So surely as you expose me, so surely will I kill you."

The man on the pavement laughed incredulously, and lifting his hat said:

"Drive on, cabbie."

Cabbie did drive on, and in intense indignation and amazement. He had recognized the man as an actor of the second class playing at one of the Broadway theaters, who had an unsavory reputation for gallantry.

"Cyril Renfrew," he muttered. "Cyril Renfrew indeed! More likely John Stubbs. So this is Cyril Renfrew's measure, is it? A blackmailer. I've often wondered where he got his money to support his pretensions. But who is she? Lucy. But

Lucy what? Hang it! I'd like to help the poor creature. But how? I cannot speak to her in this disguise, for I cannot explain. I don't care what the merits of the case may be, I'd like the chance of choking this rascal. I presume the package is a package of letters she has written him in all trustfulness, and now he is threatening to use them to her ruin if she does not give up liberally. I *will* help her, hang me if I don't. I will find out where she lives to-night, and call upon her to-morrow."

Thus were his thoughts running, when he was recalled to his amateur cab-driving by feeling the check-strap again. This time the lady wanted to alight, and so he drove to the curbstone; before he could descend from his box, she had opened the door and stepped out.. She thrust a bill in his hand, saying:

" Here is more than enough for your fare."

" But this is not Fifty-fourth street," he said in surprise.

" It is as far as I am going," she replied, and without waiting further, she darted down the cross-street, in the direction of Fifth Avenue.

Gordon leaped on the box. He had crossed to the upper corner, and so, before he could follow her, he was compelled to turn his horse and thus lost time. When he did get into the cross-street, his late fare had vanished. He drove rapidly to Fifth Avenue, but failing to obtain a glimpse of her, returned to the place where he had taken the cab.

Gordon had barely time to exchange the livery for his own clothes, when Robb drove up. He tumbled out, laughing heartily.

" By George, Jack, it is hard lines, but you've lost the wine."

" Why?" He had forgotten that Robb **had fol**lowed him.

"Why?" repeated Robb. "Because you did not drive her home, that's why. She dodged you. I saw her come out from under a high stoop after you passed, and scud down the street like a scared cat. She did not propose to be tracked by the cabman who drove her."

"I wish you had followed her," said Gordon. "Did you know the fellow she stopped to talk with on Broadway?"

"Yes, Cyril Renfrew. He's a fine whelp—universally detested—so much so that his brother actors will not associate with him. She must be connected with the profession after all."

"No," replied Jack, "I am now convinced she is not."

"What did she have to say to him?"

"Nothing pleasant, I should judge, by their tone."

"Well," replied Robb, "it's a curious adventure. But, my boy, you have lost the wine."

"Yes," Jack admitted. "We'll find the boys and buy it. Here, Herrick, here's a bill the lady gave me." He looked at it. "Hello! you're in luck; it's a five-dollar bill—two more than you expected. Good-night."

He joined his friends, and over the wine made merry; but he said not a word to indicate he had heard the conversation between his fare and Renfrew.

CHAPTER II.

ON the morning following his interview with Lucy on the street, Cyril Renfrew rose late.

After a leisurely bath, he contemplated the idea of breakfast, but as he had dined late and liberally in the small hours, he dismissed it with a grimace of disgust.

On the table in the center of the room he found a manuscript. He took it up and examined it.

"Ah! My part in the new comedy," he said aloud. " Rot, I expect. They never give me anything good if they can help it. Well, it must be studied."

He drew up an easy-chair to the window.

The apartments occupied by the actor were elegantly, even luxuriously, furnished. There was much curious and rare bric-a-brac about, of the kind one only collects after many years, and arguing for the possessor no little taste and knowledge. There were pictures on the walls evidencing artistic appreciation.

The man himself was certainly over thirty, tall, slim, and dark. His face was unquestionably a handsome one, though a keen physiognomist would not have found it attractive. Evidently giving much attention to his apparel, there was still something *outre* about it. Striking as he was, he was too pronounced to be refined, and too pretentious to be gentlemanlike.

The apartments were in a house designed for the

occupancy of bachelors alone ; consequently there were few visitors of the other sex, and such as there were created remark and unpleasant comment.

That is the reason why the janitor so partienlarly noted the appearance of a lady, closely veiled, who inquired for the location of Mr. Renfrew's room.   He remembered also, as he told upon a subsequent interesting occasion, that it was near the hour of twelve, for his wife had called him to his mid-day meal just as he turned from the lady, after having ascended the stairs with her and pointed out the door.

Renfrew, too, might have told upon the same occasion, if he could have done so, that it was not far from the noon hour, for a little French clock on the mantel chimed the half-hour after twelve, just as a rap on the door caused him to call out, " Enter ! "

'The door opened, and a closely veiled lady walked in.

The actor, rising quickly from his semi-recumbent position, bowed politely, for it was his habit to make on all occasions the pretense of great deference to the weaker sex. The lady threw up her veil, and he discovered the features of the lady with whom he had talked the evening previous.   That the actor was not pleased by the visit, he showed by the heavy frown wrinkling his brow.

" You honor me with an early visit," he said.

" Yes," replied his visitor ; " I determined to make one more appeal to you—to make one more effort to save myself from the ruin confronting me."

" You take a despondent view of things this morning," he replied.   " Since you are here, permit me to offer you a seat."

He placed a chair before her, but as she was about to seat herself in it, checked her, saying :

" It is proper for me to say to you before you sit
down, and before I close the door, that, in accept-
ing my hospitality, you are seriously compromising
yourself."

The lady bent upon him an indignant look.

" I have suffered much injury at your hands,
Jacob, but I think that in my distress you might
spare me your insults."

" Upon my word no insult was intended. I
spoke but the truth—"

" The truth," she scornfully interrupted.

" Yes, the truth. I suppose it is not testimony
as to the correctness of my life, when I say that
any woman that visits my apartments is compromised. But I should at least be given credit for
the sincerity of my motives in warning you, before
retreat in good order is made impossible."

" What is the danger of compromising myself in
this manner, compared with the ruin you are so
cruelly forcing upon me ? "

" I presume I interpret that remark correctly
when I assume that the interview is to continue
and the door is to be closed ? "

She answered by seating herself in the chair he
had placed for her.

He closed the door.

" Now then," he said lightly, " the consequences
be on your own fair head. If scandal smirches
your garments, the fault will not rest upon my conscience. Having performed my duty, let us to
business. To what do I owe the honor of this
early visit ? "

" You must surely know," said the lady impatiently. " There can be but one thing. Oh, Cyril !
I beg you not to drive me to exposure. Be careful ! Have some pity on me ! "

" ' Still harping on my daughter, eh ? ' "

" How can you be so heartless—so cruel ? Surely

I have not wronged you in the smallest way, in all my life."

" ' Necessity knows no law.' 'Where the devil drives needs must.' But I'll not vex you with old saws. It is because I must have that amount before the end of the week, or be ruined myself."

" But, Jacob—"

" Please do not repeat that plebeian name again."

" Well, then, Cyril, I have told you, and most truthfully, that it is utterly impossible for me to obtain it."

" Borrow it."

" Borrow? Where am I to borrow so large a sum as two thousand dollars? From whom?"

" A young lady so beautiful, and moving in such wealthy circles, should have no difficulty."

" You mock me."

" Indeed, I do not. Beauty in distress is powerful."

" You know I can do nothing of the kind. I have but one source of income, and that the generous allowance Dr. Sherman makes me. You have drawn so heavily upon it this quarter that I have been compelled to run in debt with my dressmaker. And I tremble lest Dr. Sherman should hear of it. I told you long ago that he had forbidden me to exceed my allowance or to contract debts."

" There are certain young and charming ladies of my acquaintance, with but one-half your beauty, who contrive to add to their incomes very considerable amounts."

The lady looked upon him inquiringly, but saw upon his face the sardonic reflection of his infamous meaning.

Intense scorn and loathing were depicted upon her countenance. She leaned forward, her face fairly livid with anger.

" You wretch !" she cried, " I would not have believed there could exist a man so despicable—so vile ! "

" See here," he exclaimed, stung into brutality by her withering contempt, " none of that. You have got to get that money, and I don't care how. It will not do for an adventuress who lives by her dishonesty to fling mud. You must not fling it at me."

" Blackmailer," she hissed at him as she stood erect.

" Yes, blackmailer if you please," he replied angrily. " But who are you who assume so much virtue ? "

" A very unhappy woman, who when a poor, weak, unsophisticated girl was urged into a wrong— a crime, by you—a crime which she has repented every one of her miserable days, and who is too cowardly to face the consequences of exposure."

" I want no maudlin sentiment," said Cyril. "The facts are plain. We conspired together to deceive that old fool. I jeopardized my own safety and reputation, and I propose to have my share of the plunder. Do you suppose I put my head in the lion's mouth, that you might revel in luxury and wealth and I not to share in it ? "

" You—you jeopardized yourself ! Yes, perhaps you did, but you took good care to recover all your letters and all evidence against yourself, while retaining all of mine. You have had your share—all of it. I conspired with a jackal—a hyena."

" Your tongue is sharp, my beauty," returned the actor. " But this interview has lasted too long. I will end it. To-morrow night by twelve I must have two thousand dollars, and, by Heaven ! I will have it. No pleadings, no tears, no bad names will swerve me from my purpose."

"You must look elsewhere than to me for it. I will not, because I can not, give you one cent."

"Then the consequences be on your own head. Friday morning your letters and a statement of the fraud will go to Dr. Sherman."

"You will commit a murder," said the girl.

"What do you mean?"

"Twelve o'clock to-morrow night will find me dead. I will not live to witness my disgrace. The act will be mine, the responsibility yours."

"Bah! You were going to kill me last night. Now it is yourself."

"Then it was passion; now it is purpose."

"Neither of your threats frightens me. You will end up by sending the money."

"Never," cried the girl passionately. "The end must come. As well now as ever. To live like this, with the fear of exposure on the one side and dread of extortion on the other, is worse than death. Then there is the remorse. Oh, how bitterly one pays for a single false step! And you, the only blood relative I have on earth—that you should treat me so!"

"Oh, let us have no acting!"

She faced him indignantly, as if about to say something more, but restraining herself she crossed the room and, placing her hand upon the knob of the door, stood a moment, her head bent. Then turning upon the actor a look of deep earnestness, she said in tones low, intense and thrilling:

"Jacob Myers, for the wrongs you have done me these five years, for the crime you urged me and led me into committing, for the wicked end you are forcing me to make, may Heaven curse you to the end of your days—may every pleasure pall on your lips, may failure attend you in everything, may your end be so sudden that you can not pray for forgiveness!"

She drew the veil over her face, opened the door, and passed out.

Renfrew watched the door close, and then shrugging his shoulders said :

"How she would capture the house, if she could do that on the stage !"

CHAPTER III.

A MODERN KNIGHT ERRANT.

ABOUT the time that the young lady he had driven the night previous was making futile effort to soften the hard heart of Renfrew, Jack Gordon was giving serious thought to her situation.

His sympathies had been greatly stirred, and he was quite young enough to have the Quixotic desire to rescue this lorn and handsome damsel from the perils by which she was surrounded.

He had nothing to do. Beyond determining upon the cut of his trowsers and the color of his coat he had no serious duties in life. A prudent and sagacious father had made this condition for him. During thirty years this father had labored industriously, amassed largely, invested safely, disposed of his business wisely, and then most considerately died, so that his son, at an age when life still has illusions, might spend lavishly.

The son was not without ability, and was indeed well educated. Had necessity pricked him, he could have made a figure in any one of the worlds an American may enter. With his money he had inherited the strong virile sense and shrewdness of his father; humor, enthusiasm, and imagination from his mother, who had died so early he could not recollect her.

That he was a young man of fashion and an idler of the town, was due more to the fact that his father had failed to urge him to a profession or an

occupation, than to predisposition—more to circumstances and associations than to deliberate
adoption. At the age of twenty-six the daily
routine of dressing and club lounging had become
irksome, the sports he and his intimates indulged
had begun to pall, and he was seriously contemplat-
ing taking to his books again. He had tried all
the means of extracting pleasure from life pursued
by his kind, and was doubting whether real pleasure
was found in the effort. He had aspirations, feeble
as yet, for something better.

His caprice for driving a cab at night was the
outcome of his idleness and weariness. It was
outside of the routine which was beginning to chafe.
He had kept it a secret from his friends, not because he was ashamed of it, but because it was
something he could enjoy apart from the rest—
alone.

The idea of rescuing the young lady fitted into
his humor. Its novelty was fascinating ; the difficulty of proceeding attractive and interesting. He
did not know who she was, where she lived, what
her name was, what her antecedents were, and
whether or not she was an adventuress quite as
much in the wrong as Renfrew. These made difficulties he burned to overcome.

But under all was the fact, that the girl had
awakened in him a great interest, had excited his
sympathies. Had he not been idle he would not
have nursed the desire to assist her, but dismissed
it with a sigh and a wish ; but being idle he nursed
it into a resolve.

Then it occurred to him that in an effort to assist
her he might involve himself in a scandal, perhaps
a crime. Discretion whispered to him to drop the
whole matter, but the idea of danger promised excitement.

As he lingered over his breakfast he balanced

inclination against discretion, and finally, with a laugh having the quality of apology in it, decided in favor of inclination, and arose from the table determined to enter upon the enterprise at once.

Indolent from habit, he was capable of great energy when moved to it. A rapid review of the conversation he had overheard the night before, and a contemplation of the end he sought, showed him how absurd, after all, was his enterprise. What did he know? Who was she? Lucy. That was all. And who was Dr. Sherman? And what relation did Lucy bear to him? And the package? What was the package? Letters presumably. It was all very vague.

He walked around Madison Square while he tried to aid himself by putting the facts in a narrative form.

"Here," he said to himself, "is a man, an actor named Cyril Renfrew, who has in his possession a package of letters, presumably, written, presumably, by a certain Lucy—who is a devilish handsome girl, by the way—which he threatens to send to Dr. Sherman—and who that duffer is I don't know—if she don't give him money, amount unknown; to send these letters to Dr. Sherman,—I wonder who that fellow is? I presume I can find out—is to ruin her. He has blackmailed her in the past. I mustn't forget that, for it is a strong point. This Renfrew is already liable. Good! There is one pin in. Now, of all the characters in this little drama I only know who Cyril Renfrew is. If Dr. Sherman is anybody, I ought to be able to find him out. Then, perhaps, I can discover Lucy. They must have a close relation of some kind, if a package of her letters in his hands can ruin her. Then if I find that out I can reach her and offer my services. That shall be the programme."

He set out upon it immediately. But a visit to

the clubs, to the hotels, to the bank parlors, to men largely acquainted with the affairs of New York and its people, failed to give him the slightest clue to Dr. Sherman. No one knew of such a person, and no one he inquired of knew a person named Lucy Sherman.

" Well," he said in one of his walks, " if I can't find Dr. Sherman, I can't find *the* Lucy. I'll have to abandon the programme. I can find Renfrew, but he won't tell me if I ask ; besides, I would have to confess I didn't know the girl. By George ! That is an idea."

He stopped short to consider it. Finally he turned, and walking briskly, said, " That's what I will do. I'll go straight to Renfrew and demand the package—I will frighten him into yielding it to me. I can do it if I am careful."

He turned into a fashionable hotel much frequented by all kinds of people, including actors. Stepping up to the desk, he asked the clerk if he knew where Renfrew's apartments were, and receiving the desired information, set out at once,— and about the time the lady was descending the stairs on leaving Renfrew, crushed by her failure.

Gordon was quite sensible of the difficulty of his undertaking ; of the tact, diplomacy, and adroitness requisite for success. He was by no means certain that he would succeed. But if he was to accomplish anything, it must be done quickly, for the lady in distress had but two days of grace, and he was possessed of an undefined fear that if he could not relieve her in time, something tragical would occur.

So he hurried on, his only plan that of frightening Renfrew by showing him that he had already made himself liable in the eyes of the law.

CHAPTER IV.

A GAME OF BLUFF.

RENFREW only knew Gordon as one of the fashionable young men of the day. He had hardly recovered from the effects of his stormy interview with the unknown Lucy, when Gordon's card was handed him. He observed it with some apprehension—a vague premonition of danger—though why he could not have told.

When Gordon entered he greeted him with a cordiality akin to effusiveness. But Jack did not respond in a like manner. He assumed that air of reserve, impassiveness and imperturbability which he had cultivated assiduously all his manhood days, as attributes of a man of the world. These airs served him well in his encounter with the actor.

"Ah, Mr. Renfrew," he replied in his coldest manner, "you would better reserve your cordiality until you have learned my mission."

Then inserting his single glass in his eye with great deliberation, he gazed steadily at Renfrew without making further remark.

The actor visibly paled under this inspection, feeling exceedingly uncomfortable—indeed, he showed it in his manner.

"Easily frightened," was Gordon's mental comment. "Cheeky, but not brave."

"Ah, Renfrew," he continued aloud, with just the suspicion of a drawl in his voice, "you are up to a very nasty game. I do not propose to have many words with you. I am commissioned by the lady whose name I shall not insult by mentioning it in your presence, but whom I shall distinguish as the one with whom you talked last night—"

" I talked with a number last night," broke in Renfrew, who had recovered possession of himself in a great degree. "You will have to be more specific."

"You will be pleased to wait until I have completed my sentence," replied Gordon. "Whom I shall distinguish as the one you talked with on Broadway last night, through a cab window. I am commissioned by Lucy—I beg the lady's pardon, for I did not propose to mention the lady's name in your contemptible presence—I am commissioned, I say, to demand that package."

Renfrew was astonished. Within the hour Lucy had left him. Neither at the last interview, nor at any previous interview, had she demanded the return of her letters. This was a new line of attack. Evidently she had gone straight from him to this man.

" Really," he said with an impudent laugh, " the lady of whose name you are so careful has selected a singular messenger."

" Yes," replied Jack calmly. " She selected one she knew would succeed in performing the mission."

Renfrew looked upon the calm, stalwart figure, and felt uneasy. He looked into the face before him, and it was impassive to the last degree.

" Oh, indeed ! " he finally sneered. " She did not inform me, when she was here an hour ago or less, that she had chosen a representative to conduct the business we have between us."

Jack needed now all his impassiveness and control. He appreciated fully the danger he stood in of betraying that he was not in the confidence of the unknown lady. What had occurred between her and the actor ? Had they composed matters ?

Had the actor granted her longer time or accepted her proposition to pay in smaller sums ? If he had, then he was not only likely to make a fool of himself, but to seriously complicate affairs for the one he was trying to assist. Perhaps she had brought the actor the money he demanded ? If she had, then he could go on and demand the letters. He must be wary, and carefully pick his words.

" May I ask," inquired Renfrew with mock politeness, " what relations you bear to the lady that she confides so delicate a mission to you ? "

" Yes, you may ask," rejoined Jack, seeking to prolong the scene, in the hopes that Renfrew would say something indicating what had passed between them. " Yes, you may ask and I may reply, that it is not the same relation borne by Dr. Sherman."

" That does not answer my question," said Renfrew with a bluster.

" Perhaps," replied Jack with calm insolence, " but it is the only answer you will receive."

" Now see here," exclaimed Renfrew, growing excited and throwing his part, which until this time he had held in his hand, on the table. " You have undertaken a contract you can't perform. You are Lucy's representative, are you ? Well, let me tell you that the agent can not succeed where the principal has failed. She came with tears, entreaties and heroics ; you come to bulldoze. Well, you will fail as she did."

The way for Jack was clear now. Renfrew in his excitement had given him knowledge of his grounds.

" No, I don't think I will," replied Gordon. " I would not be too sure. I didn't come here to fail."

He crossed the room to the door deliberately, and locking it, took out the key and placed it in his pocket. Then he placed himself in front of the door communicating with the rear room, which was

Renfrew's sleeping apartment, and looked calmly at the actor.

" What are you up to ? " asked Renfrew, angrily.

" I am going to make you give up that package," answered Gordon, carefully adjusting his glass, with a manner Lester Wallack might have envied.

" Now, my young dude," said Renfrew, both angry and frightened, " you unlock that door and go out."

" No," replied Gordon. " I don't intend to open that door and go out until it pleases me. If I do, it will be to take you with me and hand you over as a blackmailer to the police, of whom there are several on the stairs."

" Do you want to ruin her reputation ?" exclaimed the actor, thoroughly convinced that Gordon had come from Lucy because of the use of the word she had flung at him in her anger.

" No," said Gordon. " It is you who want to do that, and I don't intend you shall. Or if you do that, it shall be after you are in prison."

Renfrew, under the impulse of intense anger, suddenly sprang from his seat and rushed at Gordon with a blow, which the young man dexterously avoided, and, catching his assailant with a grip and a twist familiar to all expert wrestlers, landed the older man on his back.

" Don't try any of that with me," said Gordon, holding him down with ease. " It won't pay. You will hurt yourself." Then releasing his grip, he added, " Get up."

Renfrew, who had realized in the brief struggle the superior strength of the young man and that he was no match for him, got up sullenly and walked to his chair, where he stood glaring at his visitor, who was coolly adjusting his coat, disarranged by his efforts.

" Do you suppose I am going to give it up without value received ? " the actor said, at length.

"Yes. It's the only way you can keep out of prison."

" But I must know more about your relations to
the girl before I treat with you."

" You do not need to know anything. All you
have to do is to hand over that package."

" Well, I won't do it."

" Ah ! " said Jack, taking out his watch. " I'll
give you exactly three minutes by this watch to
make up your mind what you will do. Then, if
you refuse, I'll determine whether I will hide you
so you can not stand, or pull you downstairs to the
police. Are you ready ? Wait till the second-hand
gets at the proper place. Now."

Renfrew glared at him. The absence of anger
or emotion on the part of his visitor, his quiet determination as well as his great strength, confused
and alarmed the actor.

" One minute is gone," said Gordon with his eye
on the second-hand.

Renfrew thought he knew all the surroundings
of the girl, but the introduction of this man as her
confidant confounded him. He knew he was on
slippery ground.

" Two minutes are gone."

He feared that the girl in her desperation had
told this man everything, and if so he was in danger. He had counted on her keeping her own
secret, and now by confiding in another, and that
other a man such as the one before him, she had
escaped and beaten him.

" Three minutes are gone," said Gordon, closing
his watch and putting it in his pocket. " Now."

" I'll give it up," said Renfrew sullenly.

" You're sensible," replied Gordon. " It is of
no further value to you, and if you didn't, you
would be landed in prison."

Renfrew went to a cabinet hanging in the corner, and unlocking it, took from it a package and opened it. He stood with his back to his visitor so that the latter could not well see what he was doing. Gordon, watching him closely, became convinced that he was extracting something from the package.

Not until after he had wrapped up the package again and closed the cabinet door did he present his face to the champion of the unknown fair one in distress.

"There," he said roughly, tossing the package on the table. "You can restore them to the lady. She may well reward you for this afternoon's work. You are entitled to her favors for your service."

"I presume you mean that as an insult to both the lady and myself," replied Gordon, as he picked up the package from the table and untied it. "But it is not in your power—it is beyond your capacity—to insult any one."

Renfrew did not reply, but watched Gordon stealthily. As he supposed, Jack found a number of letters in a female hand. He carefully counted them. When he had finished, he counted them again.

"Give me the rest of the papers," he demanded.

Taken off his guard by the sudden demand, the actor replied :

"She doesn't know how many there are."

"I do ; and I want them."

"How many were there ? " sneered Renfrew.

"Don't trifle with me," said Gordon. "I'm growing angry. If you don't give them me at once I'll break that cabinet open and take them,—not only what I want, but all the letters of other women, and end your whole blackmailing business."

"Would you commit a burglary ? "

"Yes, on such a consummate rascal as you are. Come, at once ! "

He took up his heavy cane, the handle of which was solid silver, and stepped up quickly to the cabinet.

The actor quickly interposed, and throwing open the door took from it three more letters and a folded paper, flinging them at Gordon.

"There, d— you, take them."

Gordon now felt that he had secured all, and placing them with the others, slowly tied up the whole and put them in his pocket. He then took his hat, and going to the door unlocked it. As he was about to open it, Renfrew said :

"You have triumphed now. But don't think you have done with me or that the girl has."

Jack turned quickly and said :

" You are being treated very leniently. If you speak to that young lady again, or write to her, or hold any communication whatever with her, you will suffer for it."

Then stepping into the hall, holding the door open, he said :

"You are not dangerous, Renfrew. You are a fool and a coward. A fool for supposing I would bring an officer in to make a scandal for the lady— a coward for letting me bully you. When next you see me don't presume to know me ; if you do I shall be under the painful necessity of knocking you down."

The actor responded with a suppressed roar of rage, as Gordon passed out and calmly and slowly descended the stairs.

" Now," thought he, " to find the lady and restore to her the package. And I must be expeditious."

As he reached the foot of the stairs, a lady dressed in black and closely veiled stepped through the outer door into the hall. She looked about her in a hesitating manner, as if not certain which way to go.

The janitor was not at his post.

Gordon quickly judged that she was young by her figure and movements, for he could not see her features through the thick folds of her crape veil.

She made a quick step or two forward, when she perceived Gordon descending the stairs and then stopped suddenly and abruptly presented her back to him.

At this moment a lad came forth from a hidden recess, and though she spoke in a low voice Jack heard her inquire for the apartments of Mr. Renfrew.

The boy immediately led the way.

Gordon passed on to the outer door and turned to look at the lady again.

"I wonder if that is the fair Lucy returning for a second attempt?" he asked himself. "If it is, she has a surprise in store for her. And Renfrew!" He almost laughed aloud. "But I don't think it is. Lucy was taller and slighter, I think. Another victim, perhaps."

By this time the lady had reached the head of the stairs. She turned and looked back.

Gordon went out into the street.

CHAPTER V.

JACK GORDON walked up the street entirely pleased with himself. His Quixotic enterprise had terminated in the most successful manner. Now that it had been accomplished, it did not appear one-half as foolish and absurd as it did in the morning at breakfast, when he took counsel of his fears. The manner in which he had bullied Renfrew into yielding up the letters increased his own respect for himself, though he admitted that after all Renfrew was very miserable stuff. Over such a coward the triumph was not so great as it would have been over one who had made stronger resistance. Yet he supposed the truth was the actor was not without intelligence, and saw clearly that he was upon untenable ground the moment he had a man to cope with and not a woman alone, on whose fear and silence he traded. Then he made the sage reflection that nine-tenths of the women who find themselves in a similar predicament could escape their troubles by confiding in a trusty male friend. But who was the woman who entered as he was leaving? Was it the unknown Lucy? He hoped not ; yet there was something familiar in her form and voice. But who ? Then his thoughts took another direction. He must find the unknown Lucy. He would not delay a moment in this. He would make a call at once on a lady who knew nearly everybody.

By this time he had reached Broadway, and he

turned in the direction leading to his own apartments. Here he met an acquaintance who put an
end to his soliloquizing.

Mrs. Jamieson, the lady upon whom Jack proposed to call at once, was a leader in the circles of
fashion and one whose acquaintance was widely
extended. She was not only influential in the
more exclusive world of what is now called the
Four Hundred, of which she was a member by
right of birth, but she inclined herself to be agreeable to that much larger class which, having achieved
riches, was struggling for recognition. Her husband had political aspirations, and she was endeavoring to assist him.

If any one among his friends would know the
past, present, and future of New York society it
would be Mrs. Jamieson, was Gordon's idea, and
besides it was time he called upon her.

This lady was popular, and cultivated popularity.
She was of that age when she had taken on the
graces of a matron without losing the charms of
youth. She manifested an intense interest in
young people's doings, and was the recipient of
their confidences. Her pretense of motherly, or
elder-sisterly advice, was dangerously near flirtation—barely escaping it by an assumption of an
air of care and protection. To a young man, there
is nothing more fascinating than a charming matron
of thirty or thirty-five, who manifests an especial
interest in his well-being, and who chides with a
lenient eye to the follies of youth and advises with
a broad recognition of the tendencies of young
mankind.

She sought power and influence, and used such
when gained efficiently in the furtherance of
the aims of her husband, whom she devotedly
loved.

Young men were, therefore, welcome within her

doors, and as she was too sagacious to rely wholly upon her own charms, she made her parlors attractive to young girls. Her habit of motherly advice, and assumption of care of their right-going, had earned her in her own especial circle the name of " Mama Jamieson."

Four o'clock in the afternoon of this—for Jack— stirring day, found him in the parlors of Mrs. Jamieson. She came from the conservatory where his card had been carried to her, and gave him a most gracious welcome. There were, indeed, few women who did not when he presented himself.

" I ought to have punished you by sending word that I was not at home," she said, holding out to him a very pretty white and dimpled hand. " Do you know how long it is since you called upon me ? "

" If I am to measure the time by the desire I have had to see you, I should say it was years."

" Poh. That is not a pretty speech, but a very naughty one," said the little lady, as she settled herself in a low easy-chair and spread out her draperies so that they might fall in becoming folds.

" Don't sit there," she continued, pointing to one near her. " Take this seat, so that I can see your face. I am going to give you a good scolding."

" For what ? " he answered, as he obeyed her. " I am not conscious of having behaved in such a manner as to merit the displeasure of even so exacting and puritanical a person as yourself."

" Is that sarcasm ? "

" Oh, by no means."

" No, I don't think it was—only an attempt—a failure. But you shan't escape."

" Well, what is the slander ? "

" Slander, indeed. As if it were possible to slander you. Jack, you are very wicked. What do you mean by driving cabs at night ? "

Gordon laughed heartily, but nevertheless he was annoyed.

"From whom did you receive that bit of impor-tant information?" he asked.

"Do you deny it?" she asked, bending her brown eyes upon him, in which was expressed no little admiration. The wild pranks of young men excite the esteem of women.

"Oh, I never deny anything, true or false."

"You mean it is true. Don't you think you ought to be ashamed of yourself?"

"It is rather a respectable calling when followed honestly," he replied argumentatively.

"Pho! You driving a cab!"

"You think perhaps I ought to have pulled it?" said he, assuming great seriousness. "But, you see, the horse couldn't drive."

"How can you be so absurd!" said the little lady, laughing, as she laid her head back against the soft cushions of her chair, thus displaying to good advantage the outlines of her charming figure, just losing its daintiness in increasing plumpness.

"It is neither the driving nor the pulling of the cab you ought to be ashamed of. You know that.'

"Ah," he replied, in a tone of conviction. "It was wearing the livery. But cab-drivers don't wear dress coats in November on their boxes."

"You willfully misunderstand me," said his mentor. "It was that horrid bet about a defense-less woman, that you monsters should have been ashamed of. One could pass over the cab-driving in you, for you are always doing some absurdly erratic thing. But the bet."

The thought swept over Jack that perhaps her informant had been the unknown, who had recognized him.

"The bet led to no indignity to her," he said

humbly. "What is your interest in it? Do you know her?"

"No. I do not know her. Who is she?"

"I do not know. I never saw her before or since."

"What possessed you to do such a thing? Doubtless she is a lady?"

"I presume she is. Oh, I admit it was not just proper, Mrs. Jamieson, but I wanted to take 'Dizzy' Lowell down a bit."

"'Dizzy' Lowell! My precious cousin! Was he in the disgraceful affair?"

"Oh, I did not intend to 'peach' on any of them. I supposed you knew. However, I didn't take him down—I lost the bet."

"Yes, I know, but you ought to have won it. You deserved to for your ingenuity. Will Robb told me all about it to-day at the dog-show. Let me say to you, Jack Gordon, you will soon lose your reputation as being a catch if you are not more careful. Mothers will not care to entrust their daughters for life to an amateur cabman, who insults defenseless women."

"Isn't that a little hard? I plead guilty to the amateur cabmanship, but not to the insult. I suppose it wasn't nice to make a lady the subject of a bet, but you must see there was no intention or attempt to annoy the lady."

"Perhaps," said the lady, doubtfully. "If you are properly penitent I'll look over the offense and still hold open my doors to you. But you must come more frequently to confession than you have of late, or you will be stricken from my roll of eligibles."

"To find your doors closed to me would be a calamity," replied Jack with proper humility. "But to be stricken from your roll of eligibles would not be an unmixed evil."

"Indeed! You are now at the head of the list. Don't you ever intend to marry?" .

"Not so long as you confer upon me the inestimable boon of your friendship."

"Jack, you are growing audacious; are you going to become dangerous? I must marry you off. It is time some one undertook your guidance."

"Oh, don't do that. How have I offended you, that you should threaten to do me such injury?"

"Now there is another fault of yours—cynicism. It will do well enough for old men, but in a boy like you it is silly and odious. You positively must come here more frequently, so that I can correct your faults."

Gordon laughed with pleasure, by no means insensible to this delicious kind of petting.

"Yes," he said, "I presume I should go to the dogs, if it were not for your corrective influence."

"I am sure of it," responded the vivacious little woman, sitting upright and presenting to him a very pretty full face, on which the wrinkles beginning to come were skillfully hidden. "Now listen. To-morrow I am going to have a rosebud party. I did not send you cards because I wanted to punish you, and because, principally because, I was doubtful about letting you in to browse among so many pretty innocents."

"Do you think I am an ox that you talk of my browsing?"

"Be silent. That was a mere figure of speech. But, since you have been so penitent to-day, I will permit you to come. Indeed, you must come. I insist upon it. If you have made any engagements, you must break them. I command you."

"Oh, well, if you command, I must obey."

"Then you will come?"

"Certainly. Who will be here?"

"Oh, don't ask me to tell. There is my list on the table ; look that over."

Gordon took up the book with a new thought. Perhaps he would find the name of Dr. Sherman. He turned to the letter S, but could not find it. He laid the book on the table.

"Your list is a momentous affair. You do not pretend to say that you visit all these people ? "

"It is far too large," she replied, "and were not one permitted to make calls by cards, the list could not possibly be kept up."

"Are you acquainted with a Dr. Sherman ? " asked Jack indifferently, though he eagerly awaited the answer.

"Dr. Sherman," she repeated, trying to think. "The name is familiar. Oh, yes. No, I do not know him, but Walter talked of him last night as one whose acquaintance he would be glad to cultivate. An elderly gentleman, is he not? A widower? Has lived abroad the greater part of his life ? "

"I do not know. His name was brought to my attention a day or two since, somewhat singularly. Idle curiosity prompted the question."

"Ask Walter—Mr. Jamieson. He will tell you all about him. He belongs to the old Shermans up the river."

"Ah," thought Jack. "Light at last."

Before he could reply, four young ladies were ushered in, making considerable noise. Jack recognized them all—one the young wife of a prominent lawyer of the city, Caleb Van Huyn, famed for her beauty and the circumspection of her life—the three, as young ladies of society, who approached as near the standing of the "fast" young woman of English fashionable life, as American girls could and yet preserve their reputations, and known as " Mollie " Lowell, " Lou " Appleby, and " Nell " Robb.

"This is neither a descent nor an attack," said Mrs. Van Huyn to Mrs. Jamieson, who advanced to greet her. "Nor am I responsible for the appearance of these young ladies. We met at the door."

"No one ever is, the burden is too heavy," said Jack, who had not as yet been observed by the new-comers, for he was somewhat obscured from their view by an easel upon one side and a huge jar upon the other.

The voice of a man stilled the babel for a brief instant.

"It is that monster, Jack Gordon," cried Nell Robb. "No one but Jack would dare to be so saucy."

The three young ladies, with cautious tread and fingers to their lips, after the manner of "The Three Conspirators," embarked upon a voyage of discovery.

Peering around the easel, the young gentleman was found in elegant ease, nonchalantly playing with his watch-guard, staring at them blandly.

"'Mama' Jamieson's spoiled boy," whispered Miss Lowell.

"B'ess its pitty 'itty face," murmured Miss Appleby.

"Leave the child alone, Lou," said Mrs. Jamieson, who had followed only in time to hear the soothing remark of Miss Appleby. "I've been scolding him to my heart's content. He's punished enough for one day."

"I hope you are truly penitent," said Mrs. Van Huyu, but not without marked reserve in her speech.

"Penitent," cried Miss Robb. "Look at that hardened face, and ask if penitence ever sat sorrowing upon it."

"True penitence rests in the heart and not in the face, Miss Robb," replied Jack meekly; and then, with a saintly air, " There's where mine rests."

" And he pretends to have a heart," interjected Miss Lowell.

" I did, Mollie, darling, until I caught sight of that ravishing head-gear of yours, when it took flight and lodged itself in your sweet keeping— penitence and all. And Heaven knows what need you have for penitence for all your sins."

" Sins? Oh, yes ; and the last is that same 'ravishing head-gear' which has caught thine eagle eye, Jack. I stood up the milliner, and now Lowell *père* refuses to come down, because, forsooth, he says I am extravagant."

Miss Mollie took the article from her shapely head, shaking her blonde curls with a bewitching toss, and regarded the " head-gear " with affection.

" Moll," screamed Miss Appleby, " I've an idea. Go at once to papa Lowell and tell him that the ' head-gear ' has captured the immaculate Mr. Gordon, who is at your feet a tearful swain. He'll pay for seven bonnets like it."

" Do," said Jack, much interested. " He'll jump at the chance of getting rid of you so easily, and I'll—"

" What will you do ? " said the young lady, daintily smoothing the feathers of the bird ornamenting the crest of the hat. " What will you do ? "

" Jump the town to get away from you."

" I'll not have any more of such slang in my parlors. Upon my word, Mrs. Van Huyn, the way these young people talk—"

" Must remind you of the elegance of the talk in a Parisian *salon*," interrupted Jack.

" Jack Gordon, I do not—"

" By being so immeasurably unlike it," continued Jack imperturbably.

" Mrs. Van Huyn," said Mrs. Jamieson, " before

these wicked creatures came in I had reduced Mr. Gordon to a proper sort of subjection, and now—"

"And now you perceive, Mrs. Van Huyn," remarked Jack, "how 'evil communications corrupt good manners.'"

"My brother 'Dizzy,'" said Miss Lowell, in anecdotic tone, "who is rather a good fellow—"

"Much like his sister," politely interjected Jack.

"But not over-bright—"

"Wherein he is not like his sister," said Miss Appleby, her strong friend.

"Said yesterday morning at breakfast," continued Miss Lowell, unmindful of the interruptions, "that he never could understand that old proverb. 'For,' said he, 'here is Jack Gordon, whose manners are very good, but whose communications are very evil,' and in support of it he showed me a letter he had just received from you."

Jack looked somewhat foolish and a little red, so that the rest thought his antagonist had scored a point against him.

"What was it?" cried Miss Robb. "Do tell us; Jack doesn't want you to, I know, but do, please."

"No, don't," said Mrs. Jamieson. "I should be afraid to hear it, and I haven't forgotten how to blush. I'd rather tell you of his caprice of last night."

"I beg you'll not do that, my dear Mrs. Jamieson," said Jack, rising. "I could stand that letter to 'Dizzy,' but you know I've confessed and repented—surely you will grant absolution."

"You shall have it, Jack. Depend upon my discretion."

"Are you going up the avenue, Jack? We'll go with you," said Miss Lowell, teasingly. "I know, girls, he don't want us."

"Oh, I'm sure," said Jack, backing away, "I

should be delighted, but you see I've promised Mrs. Jamieson to reform and to endeavor to regain my character."

Then, making his adieus, he vanished before his impertinence could be replied to.

Mrs. Van Huyu, who had not apparently been greatly edified by this specimen of conversation, which in our latter-day civilization and refinement passes for wit, seized the opportunity to say to Mrs. Jamieson that she had called to solicit cards for that lady's " rosebud " party, for two old and valued friends.

To this Mrs. Jamieson eagerly replied that she would be greatly pleased, and asked her to give the names and addresses, which she did by laying two cards upon the table, and shortly after took her leave.

It was quite evident from the manner in which she was treated by all, that Mrs. Van Huyn was a person of consequence.

After she had left, and the girls had gathered about her, Mrs. Jamieson read the cards.

" Why," she said, " this is singular. ' Dr. Sherman.' ' Miss Lucy Sherman.' ' B—— Hotel.' "

" What is singular ? " asked Miss Lowell, laying her head affectionately upon Mrs. Jamieson's shoulder.

" Why, the moment you came in, Jack was asking me if I knew a Dr. Sherman."

" Miss Lucy Sherman," replied the young lady. " Jack must have a new ' mash.' "

" Mollie," cried Mrs. Jamieson, in supreme disgust, " why will you be so horribly slangy. Your words are not nice."

" But myself is, and so one balances the other," stopping further chiding with a caress.

CHAPTER VI.

THE PACKAGE.

GORDON hurried from Mrs. Jamieson's door with the thought that he would barely have time to dress for a dinner for which he was under engagement, and quickened also by the recollection that he had left the package he had so successfully demanded from Renfrew in the pocket of the coat he had changed before going to call.

So when he reached his own apartments his first act was to demand the coat he had worn that morning. Crimmins brought it to him, and he hurriedly searched it, under the apprehension that the letters had disappeared.

But they were where he had placed them. Telling his man to lay out his clothes for dinner, he took the package to the window and was about to make an examination of its contents.

Jack was not without a keen sense of honor, and the thought flashed over him that the letters were not his to read ; that to read them was to possess himself of a secret not intended for him. This deterred him, and he sat weighing the.package in his hand, thinking.

" No," he muttered, " it is not the proper thing to do. Should she be a lady, and it is quite among the possibilities, with a proper sense of propriety, as is quite probable, I would stand in a very poor light before her, should I be unable to say I was absolutely unacquainted with the contents of her letters. *Per contra*, I would stand very well before her. My interference into her affairs was, after all

41

is said, a piece of presumption which can be justified only by the spirit under which it was undertaken—a sincere desire to aid her to escape from
that rascal.   To read them now would be to rob me
of all the credit of that performance, would reduce
me to the level of that scamp, and beside would
place me in possession of the same power to hold
over her, whether I used it or not, and that would
put an end to all the gratitude I might naturally
expect from her.   No, I'll not read them."

"Crimmins," he said aloud to his man, "bring
the sealing-wax."

Lighting the gas, he sealed the package, saying :

"You see, I am sealing up this package after
having taken it from my pocket unopened."

"Yes, sir," replied his man, much interested in
the act, and quickly disappointed when he heard
no more of it.

Gordon, completing the sealing, placed it in a
small safe he had in his rooms, and then proceeded
with his dressing.

At the same hour that Gordon was debating with
himself as to whether or not he should possess
himself of the secret of the fair unknown, in an up-
town hotel a young woman was seated upon a rug
in front of an open fire with a small trunk beside
her, the door of her room locked.   She was weep-
ing, the tears fast flowing down her face.

The clock on the mantel chimed the hour.

She looked up and said sadly :

"The last day but one goes swiftly."

Then she again busied herself with her occupation.

This consisted of taking from the trunk letters,
old papers, the accumulations of the past five years.

As she read each one she threw it upon the fire.
Sometimes she lingered over one as if loath to
destroy it, but in the end it fed the flames.

Finally the trunk was emptied of everything save a small box. She lifted it from the trunk and opened it.

"This has been fatal to me," she said aloud. "Oh, Lucy, Lucy, your inheritance was a fatal one. But for the possession of this box I would never have been led into that miserable act. You meant it as a token of your affection ; it has become a curse. It has persuaded me into crime ; it has made my young life miserable ; it has brought me face to face with death. Little did you, or did I, think when I received it from your poor wasted hands it would bring me such evil. It is far worse than Pandora's box, for I have no hope. I'll leave it behind me."

She put it back into the empty trunk.

She sat for a long time on the rug, her hands tightly clasped upon her knees, staring into the fire. At last she murmured :

"I presume it is a just punishment for so great a crime. And yet I was so young, so inexperienced. I had but one to consult, and he an enemy who tempted me. I suppose what I ought to do is to go at once and confess everything. But I can not, I dare not. I could not endure his scorn and contempt. He has come to love me as a daughter. And he never forgives. He would turn me into the street, and I could not endure my fall. No, I prefer to die."

She rose from where she was crouching, and going to her writing-table, drew some papers before her, took her pen and dipped it into the ink.

She wrote hurriedly these words :

"Before I die—"

Then she threw her arms upon the table, and burying her head in them, she wept bitterly, her whole frame convulsed with her sobs.

A rap at the door disturbed her.

It was the maid announcing that dinner was about to be served.

"Tell my father," she said, controlling herself to answer, "that I am unwell—too unwell to dine. Ask him to excuse me."

Then she said to herself, "I must hasten before I am again disturbed."

She returned to her writing, driving her pen with feverish haste.

It was Lucy, preparing to end her life.

CHAPTER VII.

GORDON'S SENSATION.

WHEN a man of affairs has achieved something of which he is proud, he is apt to indulge himself the following morning, while lying comfortably in bed, by reviewing with satisfaction the events which have given him pleasure, before turning out to encounter again the struggle of life.

In so far as Gordon indulged himself with reviewing his triumph over Renfrew, the morning after, he was a man of affairs.

Crimmins, his valet, having looked in upon him and perceived that his "gent'man" was wide awake, brought him the morning paper, which Gordon proceeded to lazily look over.

As he ran his eye up one column and down another, his attention was arrested by the heading, "A MYSTERIOUS MURDER."

"They are always killing one another in this town," he said with a yawn. "One would think they would soon depopulate it."

The next line caught his eye,—"An Actor Killed in his Room."

"If it were that fellow, Renfrew," he continued, "it wouldn't be so bad."

He read the next line. Now his interest was fully aroused. He sat upright in his bed.

"By Jove, it is." He read hurriedly:

"Last evening," the article began, "when it was about time for the curtain to be lifted upon the performance at the—

45

Theater, the stage manager, Mr. L—, discovered that one of the actors, who bore an important part in the comedy now playing, was not yet in his room. The missing actor was not required to be on the stage until near the close of the first act, but it is a rule of the theater that every one shall be ready to 'go on,' when the orchestra is ' rung in.'

" Inasmuch as Mr. Cyril Renfrew, the name of the missing actor, had narrowly escaped responding to his ' cue ' to ' enter,' some weeks previously, alleging as a reason that he had in a nap, which he took every afternoon, overslept himself, Mr. L— feared a similar mishap had occurred, and determined to send to his room, as it was ' hard by,' as the old dramas have it. The messenger on arriving at Mr. Renfrew's room knocked, but received no response. Trying the door and finding it would open, he entered. The light from the street enabled him to see the form of a man in a chair, evidently asleep, for his head rested on his breast.   He spoke, but received no answer ; he went to the chair and shook the man, but was not heeded.   Becoming frightened he lit the gas, and found the actor was dead, a bullet-hole in his head just above the temple, from which the brain was slowly oozing.

"On the floor lay a pistol, ivory-handled.

" Now thoroughly alarmed, he made a great outcry.   A neighbor rushed in, a Mr. Tyrell, member of the Produce Exchange, and the janitor came running upstairs.   The janitor's name is William Doolan.   The messenger, whose name is Charles Crowley, hurried back to the theater with the sad tidings.

" The janitor informed the police authorities."

After giving a minute description of the room, the article went on :

" It is known that Mr. Renfrew did not leave his room at all yesterday, and when killed still wore his slippers.   He had during the day three visitors.   First a lady ; then a young man ; and finally a lady dressed in black.   Both women were closely veiled.   These persons did not visit together.   The first lady and the young man were seen by the janitor ; the young man and the second lady were seen by the janitor's son Jimmie—a bright lad of fifteen.   All are unknown.   One of the three committed the murder.   Perhaps one of the two, for it is by no means certain that the first and second women were not the same.

" Mr. Tyrell, who occupies the apartments opposite to those of the dead man, says that when he left his rooms about one o'clock in the afternoon, he heard Renfrew's voice, and the tone indicated that he was angry. This must have been during the first woman's call. Mr. Tyrell says that when he returned about half-past three or a little before, he heard in the actor's room two voices—one Renfrew's, still angry, and the other a woman's voice, and that was even still more angry.

" The boy Jimmie says that having been sent upstairs about two, or a quarter after two, by his father on an errand, as he was passing Mr. Renfrew's room he heard a scuffle and a heavy fall. Then he heard these words : " It won't pay. You'll hurt yourself. Get up.' He thought someone was skylarking."

" By Jove ! " cried Jack, much interested, " that was me."

" The boy says the tone was not angry—"

" No," said Jack, " I wasn't angry."

" and that the voice was not that of Mr. Renfrew, consequently it must have been that of his visitor, and the words must have been addressed to the actor."

" By the combined genius of the boy and the reporter," commented Jack, " an indisputable fact has been arrived at. Logic is a strong thing."

The reporter then devoted some space to the murdered man :

" Mr. Renfrew has not enjoyed a good reputation. His acquaintances say that he was perpetually in trouble with women, carrying on mysterious intrigues, and some do not hesitate to say that these were pressed for pecuniary purposes. It is thought by some that his real name was Jacob Myers."

" I could give some testimony on that head myself," said Jack, interrupting himself.

" That he was unpopular with his professional brethren is an open secret. A prominent actor, who has played with Mr. Renfrew frequently, said last night, ' Renfrew was a bad egg.' "

" I agree with the prominent actor," said Jack.

" ' He was universally detested by his brothers and sisters of the stage.' "

" I have the greatest respect for the brothers and sisters of the stage.   He was a cur," again commented Jack.

" ' I am only telling what every one knows that he had not a male friend.' "

" My respect for my species is increasing," said Jack.   " The world is not hopelessly lost."

" ' Renfrew possessed no little ability—he was more than a fair actor and had it in him to reach the higher walks, but we were all so convinced of his despicable practices in getting wealthy young girls into a compromising correspondence with him, and then bleeding them as the price of his silence, that we thought he was using a noble calling for the purpose of conducting his nefarious business, and regarded him as a disgrace to the profession.' "

" Prominent actor, I salute thee," said Jack, sitting up straight in his bed and performing a military salute, " Likewise the noble calling."

" ' If the truth is ever come at, I shall be surprised if it is not found that at last he met one who would not tamely submit and thus lost his life.'
" At all events," said the reporter in conclusion, " the affair is at present shrouded in mystery. Captain Lawton of the detective force is in charge of the affair."

" By George ! " said Gordon, " wasn't it lucky I got to him before he was killed, or her letters would be in the hands of Captain Lawton, and—By Jove ! could it have been my Lucy ? She did threaten to kill him.   Thunder !   It was to-night at midnight she was to make good or he was to send the package to Dr. Sherman.   That package, and I've got it.   Phew! " He gave a long whistle.   " By George, I'm afraid I'm in this muss.   I'll have to take account of stock.   Here Crimmins.   Come with my clothes.   Quick ! I've got business on hand this morning sure enough."

He hurried though his toilet with a reckless disregard as to what he would wear, much to the astonishment of his faithful Crimmins, and went out to breakfast and to cogitation.

Gordon was too clear-headed not to appreciate the predicament he was in. He was, in fact, a great deal troubled over the outlook. Not that he was in fear of any danger to himself, but he saw an embarrassing situation in which he thought he would not figure as a hero. The straightest way out of the difficulty, so far as he was personally concerned, was to seek the Captain Lawton spoken of in the article he had read, and tell him all, truthfully, concealing nothing. But involved in that course would be the production of the letters and the presentation of the unknown Lucy as a factor in the problem. From this course he recoiled. She might be a lady to whom this exposure or entanglement would be worse than death. He believed she was, or if he did not believe so, he hoped she was, and the hope was as influential with him as the conviction would have been. The more he considered that phase of the situation the less he was inclined to follow the course his thoughts and instinct of self-preservation suggested to him. True, he believed that she was responsible for the actor's death, but still he was not certain. There was a doubt. The truth was, he was much more interested in the fair unknown than he was conscious of.

On the other hand, he did not fail to perceive that if he were to avoid giving the information in his possession and attempted to conceal his connection with the affair, remote as it was, he would be prejudiced in the judgment of the authorities and of the public. This was the risk he ran. If finally tracked and compelled to tell his story he felt that it would not receive the credence it would, were he to volunteer it immediately. This consideration led him into an examination of the possibility of his being identified with the young man who had called upon Renfrew. The papers all said that neither the janitor nor his boy had recognized the young man. He had seen no one else in the house save the lady he met as he was going out. Neither in going to the house of Renfrew, nor in his coming away, had he met any one who knew him, until he turned into Broadway. The chances of any one thinking that he and the young man were the same were very small, was his conclusion on this head.

As to the consequences of his attempt at concealment, if he was discovered, the result was not so satisfactory. He now saw how utterly incredible his story was from the standpoint of the ordinary official and the average citizen. To satisfactorily account for his visit he would have to recite his bet, his driving of the cab, the conversation between the fair unknown and Renfrew, his resolution to assist her, and, finally, his visit to the actor and his remarkable demand on behalf of the young lady, whose relations to Renfrew he was unacquainted with, whose very name and surroundings were unknown to him.

He thought he could already hear the incredulous laugh of the city, the sarcasm of his friends. He pictured himself telling the story upon the witness-stand, and noted the skeptical laugh of the bar, the doubtful gaze of the judge on the bench, and the contempt of those practical young gentlemen of the press, who would embalm their scorn in cold type for the amusement of the public.

He cursed his knight-errantry from the bottom of his heart. Notwithstanding the reasons he adduced to himself to lodge all the information he possessed, he could not bring himself to the point of directing suspicion to the young lady in whose behalf he had involved himself. So he concluded his breakfast and cogitations with the determination to maintain silence and take the consequences, whatever they might be. He thought also he would leave town for some weeks, go south to Florida, perhaps to Europe.

CHAPTER VIII

DR. SHERMAN breakfasted at the same hour Jack Gordon did on the morning following the murder, or he would have done so had he not waited for his daughter Lucy, which he did quite impatiently. He was one of those gentlemen who, having nothing whatever to do, made a virtue of promptitude. He waited so long that he had worked himself into the belief he was ill used, and was about to send the coffee to the fire again, while he prepared a fitting rebuke for the tardiness of his daughter.

When, however, she entered, heavy-eyed and sad-faced, the rebuke died away in his concern for her condition.

" You do not look at all well," he said. " I fear you have had a bad night."

" I did not sleep at all," she replied wearily, as she took her place behind the coffee-urn.

" You are evidently ill," he said, laying down his paper and looking at her anxiously. " I must send for a physician."

" It is nothing," she answered sadly. " It will be all over to-night."

" Do you think so ? "

" I am quite certain. It is nothing serious—a headache. It is passing away rapidly."

The clock had struck the hour of nine as she spoke.

" I sincerely hope so," said Dr. Sherman, as he

returned to his paper. "You know we are to go to Mrs. Jamieson's this evening. I had quite counted on it for reasons of my own, but if you do not feel equal to it, we shall not go."

"My condition ought not to prevent you," she replied indifferently.

"I should not go without you."

"But I shall be able—indeed glad to go." The thought had occurred to her that she could escape from herself for a while.

The Doctor did not reply, but returned to his reading. His daughter poured the coffee.

As he read he kept up a running comment. "Extraordinary! Most distressing! Very mysterious!" until finally the attention of his companion was aroused.

"You seem to find something interesting."

"A very mysterious affair indeed. A murder. An actor was found dead last night—Cyril Renfrew."

The lady caught the table to save herself from falling. It was well that her father was intent upon the paper, as he would have been shocked at her appearance. She regained control of herself.

"Murdered! Last night! Why, I saw him yesterday afternoon—on Broadway," she added quickly.

"Did you know this person?" asked the Doctor, severity in his tone and scrutiny in his eye.

"As half the city did, from seeing him on the stage."

"Ah, yes. I suppose so. I believe he was popular," returning to his paper again, relieved by this reply of the lady, little knowing what it cost her to answer so indifferently.

"You saw him the last time we were at the theater," she replied. "In 'Deceit.' You were pleased with his performance, for you praised it."

" Did I ?   Was it the fellow who played the fop ?
A clever fellow.   So that is the man, is it ? "

All this time the young lady was in an agony of
desire to know more, to escape to where she could
throw off the burden of restraint.   She hardly knew
what she was saying in reply ; her head was whirl-
ing, but outwardly she was composed.

" Do you think you could bear hearing the account read ? "

" Yes," she replied indifferently.   " It will not
affect me.   On the contrary, interest me.   Read it,
please."

The old gentleman took off his glasses and wiped
them deliberately, to Lucy's torture.   At length,
having secured a satisfactory polish, he began the
same article which had caused Jack so much consideration.

The young lady listened with the most intense
interest, following each word eagerly, her lips parted,
drinking all in.   As the reading progressed, two
red spots came upon her cheeks and burned brightly ; then she grew so pale that had the Doctor
looked upon her he would have thought she needed
assistance.

Twenty times in the course of his reading she
was on the point of crying out, but by superhuman
effort she controlled herself.   When her own call
upon the actor was noted, she held her breath
awaiting the terrible announcement of her name.
When the statement was made that the callers
were all unknown she experienced a wild thrill
of joy.

Her sensations were rapid and indescribable.
Sympathy, remorse, relief, pity, satisfaction, anger,
joy, sorrow, were vividly felt, yet almost indistin-
guishably.   It seemed to her afterward as if she had
run the whole gamut of the passions and emotions.

Her father had been so much interested in his

reading that he had not observed her. When finally he read the last words, " The affair is shrouded in mystery," she cried out:

" It is horrible, too horrible ! "

The Doctor thought her words were inspired by a proper feeling, and so expressed himself, and then, seeing how pale and agitated she was, he said :

" I have been thoughtless. You were not in condition to hear so dreadful a tale."

" I trusted too much to my strength," she said. " I am quite unnerved."

" Try to compose yourself," he continued, kindly. " Try to forget what you have heard."

With this he endeavored to assist her by plunging into some gossip he had heard the night previons, and talked of the party they were both to attend in the evening.

His effort, as may well be supposed, was not successful in diverting his daughter's thoughts from the tragedy in which she had so deep an interest— with which she had so close a connection—but under its cover she was enabled to finish her breakfast, though every second seemed an hour and every minute a day.

When finally the Doctor rose from the table, he said:

" Business calls me down town, and I shall not return until late in the afternoon. While I am away try to secure some rest. If upon my return you have not recovered sufficiently to attend Mrs. Jamieson's party I will then send our regrets."

As soon as his back was turned, Lucy, carrying the paper with her, hastened to her room and, locking the door after her, devoured the account which had such interest for her.

Having finished, she gave herself up to thought. Her first feeling was one of intense relief. A great load was lifted from her shoulders. No longer would she be subjected to those demands which had made her life a torture; nor could she again be threatened with exposure; she was saved from ruin—from death. She flew to her desk and took from it the statement she had prepared, and with a wild gesture of satisfaction threw it upon the flames and saw it burn, with no attempt at concealment of her joy. Yet through all the joy, relief, and satisfaction she was conscious that this happy condition had been attained only through the violent death of her tormentor, and she scorned and condemned herself because she was happy.

Yet withal she could not repress the sense of exultation over the fact that now no one was alive who shared with her her dangerous secret, and that, with the one who had shared it now dead, discovery had become impossible. This was the one great, dominating, overshadowing thought.

As she passed out of the delirium of her joy she grew more composed and considered the other phases of the tragedy. She wondered who had committed the deed. Was it the woman who the paper said had visited him last? If so, in what relation did she stand to him? Was she another victim, who had been tortured as she had been, or worse, tortured into a condition beyond endurance and escaped from her troubles by these awful means? And the young man? Was he connected with the deed in any manner?

Then the sentiment of pity took possession of her. Forgetting her wrongs, she thought of his sudden end, in the flush of health and in the middle of a career promising success and distinction. She thought of the kindness of the murdered man to her when they were young and unstained by the crime they had committed—when she regarded him as the one helpful—her only friend.

Then there flashed upon her the remembrance of

her last words to him : "*May your·end be so sudden you can not pray for forgiveness.*"

She was stunned. What a swift, terrible realization of her impious prayer. She—she was responsible for his death. Not the woman or the man who had sped the fatal bullet. She—she who had prayed for his horrible death. She stood crouching in the center of the room, horror dilating her eyes and paralyzing her limbs. Oh, kind Heavens! Were there devils from hell who so promptly answered such wicked, wicked prayers! Oh, if she could but recall those horrible words! She was guilty—as guilty as those who killed him, for she had wished for—prayed for the end he had met.

She threw herself upon the floor, writhing in her. agony—abasing herself abjectly. Tears came to her relief, and she wept copiously.

After a while the poignancy of her grief passed away, and she fell into a condition of mental numbness in which she seemed incapable of appreciating what had occurred. She took up the paper and her eyes roved over the description of the tragedy without taking in its sense. A line caught her attention :

"The police authorities were soon notified, and Captain Lawton, the celebrated detective, to whom the discovery of the murder is confided, is in possession of the room and its contents."

Contents? Her letters? Where were they? Heavens! Did he keep them in his room? Would they be found? Were they already in the possession of the police?

Now she was thoroughly alarmed. Her senses were quickened to their full extent. The dark clouds which had been lifted from her settled down again thicker and darker than before. Now, she knew that so long as Renfrew lived and did not expose her, she had entertained a hope he

never would.   In the first flush of the new thought
she had no hopes at all.   If the police authorities
held her letters, it was but a question of time when
they would communicate the information they contained to Dr. Sherman.

She was distracted by the new misfortune.   For
a long time she could not reason upon it.   She
paced the floor nearly frantic.   She tried to think
whether the letters were signed so they could be
recognized—whether Dr. Sherman was alluded to
by name.   She hoped not,—oh how fervently !
indeed began to think so.

She flung herself on her bed in an agony of apprehension.   By and by, being exhausted by the
violence of the emotion she had undergone and the
want of sleep, she slumbered.

CHAPTER IX.

CAPTAIN LAWTON AT WORK.

WHEN. Captain Lawton was assigned to the duty of discovering the murderer of Renfrew, he lost no time in going to the actor's apartments before they could be disturbed. The body of the dead actor had been removed. In every other respect the rooms were as when the murder had been discovered.

Entering, he locked the door behind him, and lighting the gas, began his work by taking a comprehensive survey of the room.

On the floor lay a pistol. This first attracted his attention. It is safe to venture that any other man, impelled by curiosity, would have picked it up and examined the instrument by which the deed had been committed. But so far from doing so, the detective walked about it and seemed only desirous of determining its exact location upon the floor. Indeed a person of ordinary sense would have said that for a man enjoying the reputation the detective did, he was guilty of a number of childish actions ; for, going over to the chair in which the dead actor was found, he carefully examined that part against which the back and head rest, and placing himself in the chair, took a revolver from his pocket. Extracting the cartridges, he leaned his head against the back of the chair, placed the muzzle of the revolver against his temple, and then dropped his arm quickly, letting the revolver fall from his hand. It fell at the foot

of the chair and rested about eighteen inches from
it.   Leaning over the arm of the chair, he looked
from the revolver to the pistol.   Then he paced off
the distance between the two, and found that it was
about nine feet.

"It wasn't suicide," he muttered.   "The Inspector is right."

Stooping down, he picked up the revolver, and
placing himself beside the chair, facing it with his
back to the pistol, he looked over his shoulder at
it, shifted his position several times, and then
bending over and curving his left arm at right
angles with his shoulder, he seemed to be embrac-
ing something while he pointed the revolver at his
left hand.   Dropping his right arm quickly with a
swing, he let the revolver slip from his fingers.   It
fell very close to the pistol on the floor.

"Yes," he remarked again, "that is the way it
was done."

He picked up the revolver, replaced the cartridges, and returned it to his pocket.   Now he
picked up the pistol and gave it a close examination.

It was not a revolver, but a single-barreled pistol,
the like of which he had never seen.   Its barrel
was steel, once highly polished, but now dimmed
and blackened by time and neglect.   A short ram-
rod was held in place under the barrel in a groove
by loops of steel.   It was exploded by means of
percussion caps, by an old-fashioned trigger and
hammer.   The handle was ivory, elaborately carved
into diminutive nude figures of women, yellowed
by time.

"A woman's toy," he muttered, "but caused
death all the same."

A bit of thread in the head of one of the screws
which fastened the ivory caught his attention.   He
looked at it more closely, and then taking a small

magnifying-glass from his pocket looked at the thread through it.

" A bit of silk thread," he muttered.

Then turning the pistol over he noticed a slight purplish stain upon the edge of the handle.

" One of a pair," he muttered again ; " lies in a case with a purple velvet bed and purple satin lining to the cover, when at home, I'll bet."

As he was about to put it into his pocket, he lifted it quickly to his nose.

"Scented, by Jove!" he said aloud ; then, dropping his voice, " That settles it in my mind. It belongs to a woman,—patchouli."

As he put it in his pocket he said :

" Some one must go on a hunt for its mate. A difficult job, for if not of foreign manufacture, I'm a Dutchman. Looks more like a piece of bric-à-brac than a shooter."

The · floor now claimed his attention, and he overlooked every square inch of it, but his search was not rewarded.

He went to the center-table. A variety of articles covered it. A pair of gloves, not new ; a silver cigarette-case, half filled ; a few cigars ; a rumpled handkerchief ; two or three cheap editions of foreign novels ; one or two bound books ; a pocket-knife ; a portfolio, never used ; two or three play-books ; a watch and chain, the watch stopped ; a small morocco-covered memorandum book.

This the detective picked up and opened. He read a few minutes, and then drawing a chair to the table seated himself and began at the beginning.

It was evidently a statement of the actor's receipts of money for nearly two years prior. At intervals of seven days there was this item " sal. $75." These entries began on the 1st of September and ceased on the first of June.

There were other entries thus : " Oct. 17, G. F. $250 "; " Nov. 5, H. M. $100 "; " Nov. 25, T. W. $500 "; " Dec. 8, L. A. $500 ", " Dec. 15, G. F. $1000 "; " Dec. 19, L. A. $250 "; " Feb. 12, D. Dux $500."

These entries were repeated again and again, with amounts ranging from $50 to $1000 set opposite the letters, those most frequently occurring being " G. F." " D. Dux," and " L. A."

Twice the detective noticed that in the case of " L. A." the " A " had been changed to " S," or " S " changed to "A," he could not tell which. Once " D. Dux " had clearly been written over " G. F." and he observed that while " G. F." ceased to appear thereafter, that was the first time " D. Dux " made its appearance.

Having exhausted the book he laid it back on the table, saying :

" If these sums represent his receipts, then he must have had an income of nearly $10,000 a year."

The cabinet in the corner next attracted his attention. The keys were in the lock and he opened it. The receptacle was small and seemed nearly filled with letters neatly tied in packages. Nothing else. Without touching anything he looked at it a long time.

" It is very strange I can not find a single photograph of a woman in the place," he muttered.

He turned from the cabinet and went about the room as if in quest of some particular thing. He opened drawers of tables, peered into ornaments ; went into the sleeping-room and opened all the bureau drawers, and finally returned to the cabinet.

" Not a photo," he muttered.

Then he took out all the letters and carried them to the table in the center of the room, and settled himself to read them.

A rapid examination of them all showed him that the letters from one person were tied up in one package, and that they were methodically arranged in the order of their dates. All were from ladies.

He began a systematic reading of them. He took the first package at his hand.

" DEAR MR. RENFREW :

" I saw your performance of *Olaf* last night. This morning I hasten to tell you what pleasure it gaVe me. You were *lovely* and your costume just *too.* charming. Did you see me? Once I thought you did.

" HATTIE."

" MONDAY AFTERNOON.

"Your apology is sufficient and you are forgiVen. Tomorrow at three I shop at Macy's alone, and if any impertinent man with lovely black eyes should be impudent enough to speak to me on Fourteenth street, why, being *alone*, I would not dare to resent it.

" HATTIE."

" FRIDAY EVENING.

" I said no, this afternoon, but have regretted it since. See how candid I am. I am afraid it is all Very improper, but—oh, well, I shall walk on Broadway at four to-morrow—shall be in the neighborhood of Tiffany's.

" HATTIE."

" WEDNESDAY EVENING.

" I have stolen away to think over again our delicious cosey dinner all alone by our own two selves, with no one looking on. I got home, not in time to escape *mater*, who wanted to know you know, which was easily overcome, but time enough to escape questioning from *pater*. If you dare to call to-morrow, I dare to have you, only your name must be—say, say Thompson—Thompson with a P.

" HATTIE M.

"You were very, very naughty to kiss me this afternoon and ·I will never, never forgive you."

" TUESDAY AFTERNOON.

" I have thought it all over. Your plan is audacious. But if you can play the rôle of a young lad of twenty, the brother of a friend in Brooklyn (who, by the way, is in Philadelphia) can bring me home by ten at night and escape from the door without being seen, I think it can be accomplished.   I will be at Fulton Ferry, *Brooklyn* side, at three to-morrow.   Be prompt, my precious, and if you are, perhaps before we get home I'll—I'll—I'll let you kiss me.   There.

" HATTIE."

" TUESDAY MIDNIGHT.

" Most successful.   Was questioned but little.   Dada at the club.   Mama too busy with charity committee.   Sister at a theater party.   Brother out after his own tootsey-wootsey.   Oh, the bliss—the bliss of those hours.   They were all too short.   I await with impatience our next meeting.

" H. M."

The detective turned to the book and looked at the first entry of H. M.   It was of a date subsequent to that of the last letter he had read.

He continued his reading of letters indicative of stolen interviews, of assignations for the future, growing more and more unguarded in expressions of affection and passion.   Then after a long period of silence he found this one :

" MONDAY AFTERNOON.

" I can not tell you how it grieves me to refuse you anything.   I have not done it in the past, but this I can not possibly do.   I have no money and I have gotten all I can get from father or mother for a long time.

" H. M."

" TUESDAY EVENING.

" I came home from the play to find your letter.   You are exacting—nay, impertinent.   There is a tone of command that I am not disposed to submit to.

" H. M."

" WEDNESDAY AFTERNOON.

" I will meet you."

" WEDNESDAY NIGHT.

" My dream is over.   I am disilluzionized.   I know you now for what you are.   I know my danger—that you threaten me with ruin.   The end is come.   Do not try to see me or write to me.   All is over between us.

" H. M."

" FRIDAY NIGHT.

" Don't try to frighten me, for I won't be frightened. Go to my father or to my brother if you dare with my letters. Do you know what would happen ? You would be dead a second after they met you, no matter what occurred to me. Suppose you have my letters, if you should attempt to use them they would only cause your death ! What a contemptible thing you are !

" H. M."

This was the last. On this envelope was indorsed in pencil :

" Played out to the end. Can go no further. She is as bold as a lion and as brave as a soldier."

The detective read letter after letter and package after package. They differed only in form of expression. Beginning modestly they increased in warmth and finally cooled off to the financial stage, ending in pleadings, defiances, and criminations, as the various correspondents received the unfolding of his plots. In the memorandum book was found an entry of initials to correspond with the signatures to the letters. On some of the packages were indorsed in lead pencil these comments : " Worked it." " Exhausted." " Wouldn't have it." " Abject failure."

" A most methodical rascal," said the detective to himself.

There were but three packages remaining when the Captain picked up the next at his hand. On removing the elastics from it, he noticed that the first letter was of recent date, and was evidently written some time after the intrigue was in full course :

" Sept. 18, 1883.

" DEAR CYRIL :

" You must not repeat your reckless attempt to see me at my house. How could you be so imprudent ? You put me in great peril. Nothing but my presence of mind in assuming that you came about upholstery saved me. My husband is

Very suspicious and an experienced man of the world. For Heaven's sake be more prudent. Use the channels of communication we have agreed upon only, and let the written communications be as few as possible. I tremble still, from the fright you have given me.

"Dollie Dux."

A week elapses.

"Do you seek to compromise me? My husband observed your frequent glances from the stage, and commented on what he was pleased to call your impertinence in eying every pretty woman you saw. What possessed you? Do you want to advertise your capture? I will meet you this afternoon at the usual time and place.

"Dollie Dux."

Other letters followed in the same strain, and then there was this one:

"Oct. 20.

"Are you mad or am I? I can not do it. Think what you have had. The tone of your letter frightens me.

"Dollie Dux."

Then, again, two days later:

"God help me! I'll come with it, but I must pledge my diamonds to do it. Where will this lead to? You will drive me crazy.

"Dollie Dux."

A month later she writes:

"Only a few weeks of peace. You are a monster. I can not sleep, and I weep most of the day. I have gotten into such a nervous condition that I start at the slightest noise. You must stop or I shall become a maniac.

"Dollie D."

A day later:

"It is not because I do not want to, but because I can not. I have not the sum nor do I know where to get it.

"D. D."

Two days later:

"Do not do anything till I see you.

"D. D."

The next day and the day of the murder:

"I am distracted. Yes, I am in your power. I am desperate. I have pledged everything I dare to. I do not know where or how to turn. Every step I take to comply with your insatiate demands brings me one step nearer exposure. I wish I could die. Death would be a happy release. But I will see you this afternoon. Be in to meet me.

"DOLLIE DUX."

The detective hurriedly satisfied himself as to the nature of the remaining packages, and finding nothing significant in the letters composing them, returned again to those signed " Dollie Dux." He spread them open before him and studied them intently.

Finally he folded them up and rearranged them, and as he did so he said :

" That is the woman. That is the woman who killed Renfrew. She is an educated woman, of wealth and station, a timid, nervous, excitable woman driven to desperation — almost frantic through fear and nervousness. Those are the kind of women who do desperate things when goaded too far. Renfrew, my boy, you should have known that. You should have seen that it was her ruin or your death. You turned the screw of the rack once too often."

" It is not easy," he said, after stopping to cummune with himself. " It will be difficult to trace that woman. The letters do not give a clue. How guardedly she has written. The signature is evidently an assumed one. I must endeavor to find out the names of the women he associated with, and get a look at them."

He took the pistol from his pocket and placed it on top the letters, and wrapped them all up in a newspaper he took from his pocket.

Taking the bundle under his arm and placing his hat upon his head, he said aloud :

" Renfrew was killed by a woman—a married woman of wealth, station, and education, with whom he was conducting an intrigue, whom he was blackmailing, and whom he had threatened to ruin— a woman who had a peculiar pistol and may yet have its mate—a woman who signed her letters ' Dollie Dux.' That's what this night's work has amounted to."

He looked around the room. After a moment he said :

" That woman got out without any one seeing her. How it was that the report of the pistol was not heard I cannot understand. I know that the muzzle was pressed against his head, and that deadened the sound, but surely some one ought to have heard it. I'll inquire into this."

He went into the hall and called the janitor.

" Who occupies the rooms adjoining those of Renfrew ? " he asked.

" Mr. Steele."

" Who is he ? "

" A lawyer."

" Was he in his room this afternoon ? "

" No, he is in Washington—went day before yes- terday, and isn't back yet."

"Was anybody there ? "

" No. I have his keys."

" Who has the room above ? "

" Mr. Downing."

" Was he in ? "

" No, sir, nor any one else. You see it was at a time of day when the gentlemen were about their business."

" Yes, I presume so. What is below ? "

" A doctor's office. It isn't occupied."

" Who has that room ? " pointing to one on the opposite side of the corridor.

" Mr. Tyrell. He was in about that time, and is now."

" I'll call on him."

He rapped on the door and was admitted.

Mr. Tyrell, however, had not heard an explosion when he returned about half-past three o'clock. While stopping to unlock the door he had heard the angry tones of Renfrew's voice, and the agitated tones of a woman in reply. He had not paid attention to it, for it was not uncommon to hear such things in Renfrew's rooms. Knowing him to be an actor he thought a rehearsal was going on. Indeed, Renfrew, after an unusually noisy time a year previous, had told him so. After entering his room he had gone to his bath, which was in the most remote part of his suite. The shot might have been fired while the water was running, or, indeed, after he had gone out again, since having bathed he dressed, and went out immediately.

All effort upon the part of the detective failed to elicit from the janitor and his son anything like a description of either of the two women who had called on Renfrew, for they were both so closely veiled that their faces were not to be recognized, and as to the young man they so flatly contradicted each other as to his dress and appearance, the Captain began to believe that not less than two had called upon the dead actor before the visits of the two women.

It was now not far from midnight, so he went to his rest.

Early the next morning he began an industrious inquiry among the associates and acquaintances of the murdered man. Here apparently the way was as dark as in any other direction.

These were the facts he elicited :

Renfrew had not a single intimate in his profession.

No one could suggest the name of any man with whom he was on terms of intimacy—he had been dubbed in the profession " The Lone Star."

No one could suggest the name of a woman with

whom he was acquainted or was intimate.   He had at long intervals been seen on the street with some, but who, none could tell.

No one knew anything about his antecedents, where he came from, where his family was, or to what country he owed nativity.

A vague tradition existed that his right name was Jacob Myers, but no one could confirm it, and it was disbelieved, although doubtless " Cyril Renfrew " was a *nom de théâtre.*

" Most mysterious," was the Captain's comment on this result.   " It grows thicker and thicker.   I'll go to the Inspector, make him understand the difficulties, and hear what he has to say; then I'll write up my report."

CHAPTER X.

CAPTAIN LAWTON'S VISITOR.

THE detective had not been long at the report, the writing of which he had promised himself that afternoon, when an attendant announced that a lady wished to see him.

"Who is she?" he asked, looking up from his writing.

"I don't know."

"Didn't she give you a card?"

"No; she said you wouldn't know the name."

"Admit her."

A richly clad woman, closely veiled, speedily followed on his words.

The Captain greeted her with a courteous bow, and placed a chair for his visitor, who probably did not notice that it was so placed that the light fell on her face, while the detective was in the shadow.

"Do I address Captain Lawton?" the lady asked in a sweet, low voice, which trembled either with agitation or timidity.

"Yes, madam. Please take this seat."

She took the chair indicated, and began to nervously remove one of her gloves.

The detective waited for her to make her business known. While waiting he rapidly concluded that she was young from the outlines of her form, of the higher walks of life from her air, and rich from the diamonds sparkling upon the white fingers of her ungloved hand.

Evidently she was greatly embarrassed, and foı a long time did not speak.

The Captain did not assist her. In this he **was** governed by purpose.

Finally, she timidly ventured the remark :

" I find myself in an unpleasant predicament, and I thought perhaps you might assist me."

" I am at your service," replied the Captain. " To whom have I the honor of talking ? "

" Is it necessary that I should disclose my name ? "

The Captain smiled.

" I imagine I shall not be able to assist you much if I am compelled to walk in the dark."

" Perhaps so."

After some hesitation, during which she drew off the other glove and nervously rolled and unrolled the two, she continued :

" Some years ago I was guilty of a foolish indiscretion which has brought me into much trouble. My father is a stern man, strict in his ideas of propriety. The indiscretion was a silly flirtation with a man, who, having received letters from me, threatened to use them to my disadvantage if I did not pay largely for his silence."

" I wonder if this touches the Renfrew case ? " thought the detective. Aloud he said :

" And you want me to compel him to discontinue his persecutions—to make him yield up those letters ? "

" The persecutions are discontinued, but I would like to have the letters."

" Who is the person ? "

" Must I tell that ? "

The Captain smiled at her innocent question.

" If I am not to know the name of the person who wrote the letters, nor that of the person to whom they were addressed, I can not see how I can assist you."

"He is dead."

"Oh, then they are in the hands of some one, you think?"

"Yes."

"The name of that person, then?"

"It is yourself."

The Captain became much interested. "What a little idiot she is," he thought, "not to see that I already know the name of the man!"

Aloud he said:

"Oh. If I do not possess them," he said blandly, "I know where they are."

"But you do not know who the man is, for I have not told you."

"Pardon me, I do. The man was Renfrew, the actor."

The woman started with surprise and alarm.

"Are you a wizard?"

"Not at all. The only letters in my possession addressed by a woman to a man who was black-mailing her, are those addressed to Renfrew. And Renfrew is dead."

"Then," said the lady, "while I was carefully concealing the name, I was telling you?"

"Yes," replied the detective, smiling, "and you come to me because of his murder."

"Why, how do you know?"

"It all follows from the first. You read the account of his murder, you saw that the case had been placed in my charge, you feared that the letters coming into my hands would be made public, and you would be exposed. Is it not so?"

"Yes," replied the lady, apparently overwhelmed with surprise at the rapidity and accuracy of his conclusions. "Since you know so much you make my way easier. Won't you give them to me? They are signed Lucy. That is all, I am quite sure."

"How long is it since his persecutions ceased?"

asked the Captain, paying no heed to her request.

" Only with his death."

The Captain muttered to himself, " Can this be
the woman ? "

After a moment's thought he partially rejected
the idea, for he reasoned that a woman who had
done the deed would not go straight to the man
who was searching for the murderer.   Then he
wished she would lift her veil so that he could look
at her face.

Aloud he said :

" So recent, was it, indeed ? "

" Yes," she replied, and the ice being broken she
was more at ease.   " You will have no difficulty in
determining them.   I am not certain, of course,
that you have them.   I do not know whether he
kept them at his rooms or on his person."

" You say they were signed—" stopping to have
her pronounce the name.

" Lucy."

" That is your name ? "

" Yes.   They were foolish, silly letters."

Then she thought, " If he has read them, he will
know that is not true.   Perhaps he has not ; if he
is a gentleman, and he looks like one, he has
not."

The Captain would have laughed heartily could
he have read her thoughts, but he was thinking
less about the letters than of her relation to the
man and the deed.

However, he stretched forth his hand and took
from the desk the sheet upon which he was writing
when he was interrupted by her entrance, and examining it carefully, replied :

" There were no letters found signed ' Lucy.'
You are quite sure they were so signed ? "

" Quite," she replied, as she threw the veil from

her face, disclosing a pair of very earnest eyes and features of rare beauty.

"What do you suppose he could have done with them?" she queried appealingly.

"That woman never committed the murder, I am quite certain," he said to himself.

He laughed as he said to her:

"You credit me with knowing more than I do. Had he any other place where he deposited his valuables?"

She looked at him wonderingly, and replied quite innocently:

"I do not know. I knew nothing of his life or habits. Do you suppose he could have sent them to my father?"

"Perhaps if I knew your father I might be able to judge," replied the detective, trying his hand at a little fishing.

He was disappointed.

"No," she said, thinking aloud, "he could not have done that, for I would have heard of it before this."

The Captain thought to take her by surprise and obtain an admission from her which he could follow up to his advantage.

"Did he have them when you saw him yesterday?"

"Saw him yesterday," she repeated. "How do you know I saw him yesterday?"

"I did not know it until this moment. At what hour did you call upon him?"

Lucy hesitated for a time, nearly overcome by what she considered the supernatural shrewdness of the man, and not a little awed by his masterfulness.

"Between twelve and one—about half-past twelve," she replied.

"Who were the young man and lady who called after you?"

" I don't know."

There was the same wondering expression on her face as when he asked if she knew whether Renfrew had another place where he left his valuables, as if she were surprised at his question, and the expression caused the detective to believe that she was innocent of any complicity in the deed.

" Did you ask him for the letters ? "

" No, I did not."

" What did you go to see him for, then ? "

" To beg he would not demand the sum he requested and not send the letters to my father."

" What was the sum he wanted ? "

Lucy now began to appreciate the blunder she had made in going to the detective, for she feared his questions would lead to a revelation of her secret. She was put on her guard by the thought, and she summoned to her aid all her intelligence.

" It was two thousand dollars, and I did not have it and could not get it."

" A large sum," said the detective. " What did he say to you ? "

" He laughed at me and told me I must give it to him by to-night, or he would send my letters to my father ? "

" What did you reply ? "

" I told him that he would drive me to kill myself,"

" You must have felt relieved when you saw that he was killed ? "

The detective had asked this question deliberately, and he watched her keenly as she replied ; he noticed that her face reddened.

" I was very wicked over that," she replied, " for the first sensation was relief and gladness, but the thought was soon lost in the fear that exposure would come from another source."

The Captain thought as she looked at him,

shame, not remorse, expressed on her face, that she certainly was not the woman.

" When did you write your last letter to him ? "

" About four years ago."

Now it was the Captain's turn to be surprised.

" How did you communicate with him ? "

" I never did unless he wrote to me, demanding that I meet him and bring him money."

" Where did you meet him ? "

" Usually on the street or in the park."

" Have you been giving him money all these four years ? "

" Yes."

" Such large amounts ? "

" Oh, no. The largest he demanded before was five hundred dollars, and that only once. He usually asked for half that amount. I never wrote to him after I saw the use he put my letters to."

" You have his letters demanding money ? "

" No, I burned them as I received them. I was ashamed and afraid to keep them."

" Now, isn't that just like a woman ! " said the detective. " Why, my child, the first one was your protection, and a threat of exposing him for blackmailing would have silenced him for ever. He traded on your fears and innocence. Didn't you ever visit him at his rooms ? "

" Never until yesterday."

" Where did you first meet him ? "

Lucy had been able to answer him truthfully until then, but now she could not do it. Her quick intelligence told her she must make an answer of some kind, and she parried to gain time.

" Must I tell that ? " she asked appealingly.

" I think it would be far better," he replied gently ; " I am not asking these questions from idle curiosity."

" But it is humiliating," she replied.

" Telling me is like talking to your father-confessor, your physician, your lawyer," he said assuringly, if not truthfully.

His untruth was met with another even more adroit.

" If ·I must I suppose I must.   I saw him on the stage, and was silly enough to write him how much I admired him.   I did this two or three times, and then I gave him an address and asked him to reply. He did so, and after a while he asked me to meet · him on Broadway, wear a red rose on my coat, and he would do the same. `We did, and the flirtation began."

" Oh, the silly moths of girls ! " commented the detective, well satisfied. " That was how long ago?"

" Five years."

" And you were how old ?"

" Seventeen."

" You have paid dearly for your folly."

" I have, indeed."

" Do you know of any one who called herself ' Dolly Dux ' ? "

" No," again with that wondering expression.

"Did you know that Renfrew treated other women as he did you ?"

" No, I supposed I was the only one."

The Captain said to himself that she was evidently an innocent, and that he had extracted all he could from her, and he would close the interview.

" You have not given me your name yet ? "

" Since you have not the letters I do not think it necessary. You can not help me, you see."

The Captain smiled.

" Oh, that is as you please, of course."

His visitor prepared to depart.

" If these letters were to come into my possession, I would not be able to communicate with you."

She drew her veil over her face, saying as she did so :

" Oh, I shall call on you again in a week. If you should find them retain them until I come."

The Captain smiled again, and, bowing politely, accompanied her to the outer office.

Two or three un-uniformed men were lounging in the room, to one of whom the captain made a rapid signal.

He conducted his visitor to the outer door, bowed her out, and then turning quickly to the man, who had followed him close behind, said :

" Follow her, don't let her get out of your sight ; tell me what her name is and where she lives."

Returning to his private office, communing with himself he said :

" No, she has had nothing to do with this murder. She is a girl standing in great fear of her father, dreading exposure of what, doubtless, is something worse than mere flirtation—something which she is repenting, moved thereto by Renfrew's successful blackmailing. However, I must keep her in sight. She may prove useful before I am through with the case."

Lucy drove back rapidly to her hotel, little dreaming she was followed, much disturbed and perplexed by the disappearance of her letters. She felt her condition was worse than before. She knew from what quarter she might expect danger before, and could, perhaps, guard against it ; now she could not tell from whence the next blow would come, and she could not arm herself at all points. Life seemed dark and drear ; there was no joy in it.

CHAPTER XI.

THE ROSEBUD PARTY.

THE vicinity of Mrs. Jamieson's house in Madison Avenue bore an air of festivity on the night of her rosebud party. Lights flashed from every window of her mansion, and as the doors opened, which was at frequent intervals, there issued forth the sounds of music, of the happy babble of voices, and the fragrance of many flowers. Carriages lined the street on either side, and a tall policeman was ordering their coming and going, as well as keeping the carpeted pathway across the sidewalk under the awning clear of the children and servant-maids who thronged on either side.

As Gordon's carriage drew up at the curbstone, he roused himself from his contemplation of the embarrassments in which his foolish knight-errantry seemed to have involved him, and the possible consequences of which weighed upon him more and more as he dwelt upon them.

He opened the door of his carriage, and as he stepped out, he said to himself : " I'll keep my promise to Mrs. Jamieson, and then leave the town for some months."

When once in the room assigned to gentlemen, he found, among others of his acquaintances, several of those who were present at the time he had made his wager with Dizzy Lowell.

Will Robb, who was struggling with a refractory cravat before the glass, saw him enter, and cried out :

"Hev a keb, sir. Tek you up for a dollar 'n hef."

The story of Jack's exploit had evidently gone abroad, for his ears were saluted with the cry taken up by every one in the room.

In view of the trouble he felt he would probably be involved in through that exploit, the chorus was not particularly agreeable, but he well knew that a display of the slightest annoyance would be a signal for persistence, and so he fell into the spirit of the fun with all the grace he could summon.

The joke, therefore, was soon exhausted, but he was compelled to undergo what was still more disagreeable—the admiring comments of the callow youth who saw something dashing and heroic in his adventure.

From these he escaped in time, and prepared to descend to the parlors. While doing so, he said to Will Robb, who was loitering behind the rest, apparently waiting for his friend, with some sarcasm:

"You owe me considerable, Will."

"Owe you what? Owe you nothing."

"An opportunity to be for once entertaining to Mrs. Jamieson."

The young man reddened slightly as he replied :

"Come again. I don't catch on."

"Oh, yes, you do."

"You mean my telling 'Mama J.' of that cab-driving bet? The joke was too good to keep. What do you care?"

"I don't say that I do care, but your tongue swings too easily, my lad. One day it will swing off, and then there'll be none."

By this time he was ready, and they descended the stairs together.

The scene in the great parlors was attractive and inspiring. Crowded rooms were indeed not unusual at Mrs. Jamieson's social occasions, but in this

case there were a large number of fresh faces—
débutantes of the new season,—the "rosebuds."

They stopped a moment to look over the
scene.

" Extraordinary good ' browsing pasture,' " said
Gordon. Robb looked at him in surprise. He did
not understand the allusion.

Mrs. Jamieson was standing near the door, and
the two young men presented themselves.

" Here are two scapegraces," was the greeting of
that lively lady. Then to Gordon she said, " I began to think you would fail me. You are late."

" Not very, I think. You see I am preparing to
leave town early to-morrow."

" To leave town at the beginning of the season?
What folly is this? "

" Having been awakened to the awful wickedness
of my life by your admonitions, I am going into
solitude for repentance."

" You repent ! " The lady's face was a picture
of fine scorn.

" What," inquired her husband, " has the little
woman been lecturing you? "

" Lecturing me !" repeated Gordon with doleful
air. " The term fails to convey the slightest idea
of the drubbing (verbal, I mean) she gave me yesterday."

" What for? What have you been doing? Oh,
I know, the cab-driving scrape."

The host laughed heartily.

" Oh, it was not that alone," cried the little partner of his life. " It was the general uselessness of
his life. But don't stand idling with me. There
are hosts of pretty girls in the rooms, who need
some one to teach them the way they should go
this season."

" There, Will, there's a *carte blanche* for you,"
said Gordon. " Mrs. Jamieson lets you loose alone

in this garden of roses. She positively trusts you to behave yourself."

"It is not Will Robb I'm troubled about," replied the lady, "it is you. Still, if you are going away to-morrow you can not work much harm. So run along like two good little boys."

"Come, Jack," said Robb, putting his arm through that of his friend, "we'll look over the 'buds' and make our selections."

They moved off before the vivacious hostess could reprove him for his impudent speech.

The young faces about them were to a great extent strange, for they were nearly all those belonging to débutantes, sipping the sweets of their first season. Such of the guests as they recognized and saluted were what Robb irreverently called " old rounders," by which he meant those who had been out more than one season.

Jack was as much displeased as astonished to find what a hero his amateur cabmanship had made of him, and how widely the story had been spread. He heard allusions to it from every side, and though he bore up under it bravely he was heartily ashamed of himself.

The two young flowers of the fashion and chivalry of Gotham had made their way down the long parlors, when Jack saw two young ladies with whom, to use his own phrase, he was "very chummy," and who are not strangers to the reader, standing just inside the conservatory; dropping Robb's arm he hastened to them.

As he drew near them he saw a face whose beauty at once attracted him. The lady sat in a corner easy chair, a picture of elegant, indolent grace. On one side, near the conservatory door, sat a distinguished-looking gray-haired gentleman in earnest conversation with Mr. Van Huyu, a celebrated lawyer of the city ; on the other side, engaging the attention of the lady, was a young gentleman who Jack knew was an *attaché* of the State Department at Washington, and who was quite evidently much fascinated by his fair companion. And well he might be, for, surrounded as she was by Gotham's fairest daughters, she outshone them all. ·

Exquisitely attired, her costume was a triumph of art and displayed her magnificently developed figure to its best advantage. She was a brilliant and striking figure, with her dark hair, soft, large black eyes, quickly responsive to every thought flashing across her mind, her brown, velvety skin, through which the color showed as clearly as if it had been fairer, and her high, regular, and finely chiseled features.

Notwithstanding her indolent *pose*, Jack observed that her face betrayed a feverish animation and that her eyes were unnaturally bright—that she seemed to breathe through her slightly parted lips as if she were oppressed.

All this he had rapidly taken in while he was making his salutations to his friends, who were two of the class Will Robb had so elegantly termed " rounders." They justified the application of the term by the vociferousness of their greeting of him.

" Now not a word about it, please," said Jack. " I know you are burning to say it, but do earn a continuance of my unbounded affection for you both, by refraining from a word of mention of it. You know how ardently and devotedly attached I am to both of you, and I assure you it is largely due to your never saying what the rest of the world does."

The two young ladies stared at him in amazement.

" Methinks," said the blonde in a diaphanous mass of pink, who was Miss Lowell, with a pretty affectation of solicitude, " methinks, Jack, thou hast found thy way to 'Mama Jamieson's' wine before the rest of us."

" Yes," added the brunette, with saucy, tip-tilted nose, her sworn friend, Lou Appleby, " Yes, and hast addled that poor pate of thine."

"Spare me," answered the unabashed Jack. " I can stand everything but the slings and arrows of your wit. The increasing loveliness of both, double-barreled as it is, I can, perhaps, because I am getting accustomed to its glare. Mollie, that's a very becoming gown you have," he continued, surveying the blonde with an approving air through his single glass. " A little too much up in the back."

" Up ! " cried the other, stricken with envy over the compliment to her friend. " Too much up in the back ! Goodness, Jack, one must wear a waist!"

" Oh, must one ? " retorted Jack, turning his monocle on the fair speaker. " Where's yours then ?"

"You are impertinent, Jack, my dear boy," was her reply. " You are not improving a particle, notwithstanding all our pains. I think it must be the night air."

" Yes," assisted Miss Lowell, " taken from the box of a cab."

" There, I knew it," rejoined Jack, sorrowfully, " I knew you would forfeit my affection before you finished. I felt it when I came up. I warned you in time too. It is too bad."

" What's too bad ? " cried both in one voice.

" The thoughtless way in which you manage your unruly tongues. But for that fatal defect both of you long ago might have been Mrs. Gordon."

" Both ? Oh, horror ! "ejaculated Miss Appleby. " It would be horrible to be the whole Mrs. Gordon, but to be a half—"

"Well, I should think it would be better," replied Jack argumentatively. "You see it would mitigate the evil just fifty per cent."

"You are not wholly lost, Jack," said Miss Mollie. "You have a proper appreciation of your own value. Yes, it would be an unmixed evil in whole or in part."

"An unmixed evil, eh?" inquired Jack with suspicious compliance. "Yes, I think so myself—for me."

The only way in which the young ladies could show their resentment was by immediately presenting their backs to him with their noses inclined upward.

Jack attentively regarded their backs.

"Oh, yes, yes. The drapery is very fair. Do it yourselves?"

They came about with the precision of soldiers, profound disgust on their faces.

Jack turned slightly, and again observed the lady in the corner chair.

"Who is the lady flanked by Winter and Spring and confronted by Autumn?" he queried.

"Why do you ask?" demanded Miss Appleby.

"That you may desert us?" inquired Miss Lowell.

"That I may know who she is—surely a simple reason?"

"Far too simple and guileless," rejoined Miss Appleby. "But I shall exhibit no petty spirit of envy. I'll tell you all I know. She is a lady with whom I have no acquaintance."

"Your knowledge is extensive. Does yours have the same breadth and depth, Mollie?"

"I can say without hesitation it has."

"The youthful cavalier fresh from the halls of Washington," resumed Miss Appleby, "seems to be captivated—to be mashed, so to speak."

"Yes," said Jack. "He appears to be making his running under whip and spur."

. "Fascination for the whip," said Miss Lowell.

"And desire to please for the spur," added Miss Appleby.

Jack opened his eyes with mock surprise.

"Why, your wits are brightening."

Before either could punish him for his impertinence, one of the young guests—and very young and conscious—came up with a blush and a stammer, and claimed the hand of Miss Lowell for a dance.

"I say, young Nettleton," said Jack, with a drawl, "are you going to dance with Miss Lowell?"

"If she will do me that honor."

"I suppose your life is insured, but run out and get a policy on your heart. She's dangerous. I know it, to my sorrow. You see in me the wasted victim of an unrequited passion, of which she is the object. She lives but to slay."

The lady rewarded him with a delicious *moue*, and walked away with her blushing cavalier.

"Jack," said Miss Appleby, "give me your arm and take me to mother. The dear old girl has been quite reasonable so long as Mollie was here, but I see the clouds gathering. Your reputation is so bad, I can not endanger mine with talking to you alone, and what is far worse, put myself in peril of a scolding for having encouraged that very disreputable person, Mr. Jack Gordon."

"Ah," replied Jack, as he offered her his arm. "I begin to doubt whether a life of virtue and extreme piety is its own reward. But the truly good always were slandered from the beginning of time."

The young lady's mother did not seem to regard him with great horror, however, when he brought her daughter, for she greeted him with a smile.

Jack was glad to escape, for all the time he was

indulging in persiflage with the two young ladies, he was giving much attention to the one in the corner.

He sought Mrs. Jamieson at once.

" Well, you naughty boy," said she, as be came up. " I've been watching you. You have devoted yourself wholly to that flirting cousin of mine and her friend Lou, both of whom know well enough how to obtain attention without monopolizing one I intended for a lieutenant. See how nobly Will Robb is doing his duty."

" Yes, I know. He is a model. But it is reserved only for a few to attain the altitude pf his goodness. He resembles an angel."

The idea of Robb's resemblance to an angel was too much for the jolly little dame, and laughing, she tapped him on the shoulder with her fan, saying :

" I give you up. You are incorrigible."

" Don't do that, please. Because I want you to do me a favor."

" And what may that be, please ? "

" Tell me who is the striking lady seated in the corner ? "

The lady looked in the direction indicated.

" Why," she said, " that is the daughter of the gentleman you inquired about yesterday—Dr. Sherman. That is he sitting beside her, the old gentleman. It is Miss Lucy Sherman."

" Will you not present me ? "

" No, I will not, for you don't deserve it. But I'll compromise with you. Here's Mrs. Van Huyn, she is Miss Sherman's chaperon. I will ask her to present you."

Then turning to Mrs. Van Huyn, who was seated near her, she said :

" Mrs. Van Huyn, here is a sighing swain who desires to be presented to your charming charge. Will you not do it for him ? "

The lady, who was moodily listening to the dron-
ing of an antiquated beau, who vainly imagined he
was making himself most agreeable to a pretty
woman, rose, her face brightening, and took the
proffered arm of Jack.

The young lady was still listening to the engaging young diplomat.

" Lucy, my dear," she said, " Mr. Gordon desires to be presented to you.   Miss Sherman."

The gentleman from Washington, loth as he
was to relinquish his seat, disappeared with a bow,
and Jack dropped into the chair just vacated.

He had found the unknown Lucy.

CHAPTER XII.

WEB SPINNING.

L UCY received Jack graciously.
To be received graciously, however, was nothing new to Jack. All women gave him a welcome. He had a winning personality, even if he could not boast a handsome face. His manner was deferential, yet self-assertive ; his demeanor modest, yet bold. He accepted every woman as an equal—neither as a superior nor an inferior. While thus flattering them without an air of condescension he compelled respect for himself without becoming a prig.

After the ordinary nothings with which strangers begin conversations, Jack remarked that he imagined Miss Sherman was not a resident of the city.

" No," she replied, " we do not count ourselves residents, though, as a rule, we spend the winter months in town. We live at Caldwell."

Jack expressed surprise at not having met her before, since, as he said, he went about a good deal.

" It is not strange," she answered. " Last winter I did not go out because of the death of an aunt who lived with us. The winter before we were in Europe."

It should not be forgotten, that while Jack was making himself agreeable to Lucy, he firmly believed he was talking with one who had caused the death of Renfrew, and he marveled over her composure and self-command. The feverishness, the suppressed restlessness, he had noticed when he first observed her, were still present in her manner. To be sure the indications were slight, and indeed, if Jack had not been looking for manifestations of the awful experience he felt quite certain she must have passed through during the preceding twenty-four hours, he probably would not have perceived them. Of all this he was aware, and he wondered how a girl so young, and who did not bear upon her countenance visible expression of the possession of such qualities as would urge her to commit such a deed, could carry herself with such perfect self-possession.

He covertly studied her. He saw a strong, refined face, showing capacity for emotion, for passion even, instinct with intellect. That it was the face of one who could, in a moment of intense anger, made desperate by great wrong, strike a deadly blow, he could well understand. But he could see no cruelty in it ; on the contrary, there was much sensibility apparent, and the mouth, well formed and firm as it was, manifested large power for affection. Her eyes, dark and glowing, were neither hard nor cold, but soft, luminous, and responsive.

How she could have brought herself to attend a place of festivity, to carry herself with so much composure, and to engage even in the light, trivial conversation they were making, puzzled him. He took refuge in the trite consideration that women were not to be comprehended by the male biped.

Notwithstanding all he knew of, or thought he knew of her, he found himself greatly attracted. This might have been accounted for by her beauty, but Jack would not admit it to himself, for he thought he had discovered a strength in her, the suggestion of a latent power in all she said, however trivial, which fascinated him. Then, too, her voice, which was her richest gift, was low and soft,— a quality in women to which he was partial.

There was another thing which puzzled him, for it seemed a contradiction. She had won his re- spect. He knew that he never could, however long he might know her, or however intimate he might become, get upon the same terms he was with Mollie Lowell or Lou Appleby. He could not picture her engaging in the sort of chaff he had had with his two friends earlier in the evening.

In short the girl, the deed, and her after-conduct were irreconcilable. He abandoned the effort to understand her, without abandoning the belief that she was the slayer of Renfrew. He gave himself up to the thought of how he could communicate to her the possession of her letters, and to her fasci- nations.

No doubt Jack is presented in an exceedingly reprehensible light. No doubt if Jack had been a model young man his soul would have revolted at the idea of talking with, much less endeavoring to impress himself favorably upon, one he thought guilty of life-taking. No doubt if Jack had been the proper sort of young man he would have imme- diately communicated the knowledge in his pos- session to the police, and thereby made a fool of himself. But not being a proper sort of young man, he escaped being a fool, and as this pen is not constructing a model, but is striving to present, too feebly it is true, a typical young man of New York of the nineteenth century, perhaps having a little too much heart, intellect and enthusiasm, but not too much shrewdness or premature sagacity to be typical, it can do no more than set down the facts.

Now that he was in the situation he had so earn- estly desired, face to face with his fare of three nights previous, he could not find a way to convey his information. He had already determined to make himself an accessory to her crime, although he did not use that ugly word, nor regard his act in such a light, by concealing all knowledge he possessed. He meant to deliver to her the letters, convince her he did not know their contents, and make her fully comprehend that she had nothing to fear from him.

There was, after all, something chivalric about all this. He had no ulterior purpose. Indeed, he would have revolted at the idea of gaining advantage by the possession of such power. He might have desired to win the girl, but his triumph would have been valueless in his eyes, had it been achieved by such means.

All this time they had been chatting, and Jack had made no progress in discovering his possessions.

Dr. Sherman, who had been absorbed in conversation with the distinguished lawyer, now rose and said to Lucy:

"Come, my dear. You have not been well for a day or two, and you must not overtax yourself."

Lucy rose with prompt obedience, and Jack and the lawyer did the same.

At this moment Mr. Van Huyn engaged the attention of Dr. Sherman by a further remark, and Jack was enabled to say:

"I have been greatly pleased to make your acquaintance, Miss Sherman, and dare to express the hope that it will not cease with this meeting."

If he had hoped by this cast to catch a fish he was disappointed. Lucy contented herself with a courteous inclination of the head in acknowledgment.

However, Jack was not to be defeated without due effort.

" Shall I be transcending the proprieties," he persisted insinuatingly, " in asking to be permitted to call upon you ? "

Lucy did not seem to be outraged by the proposition, yet she hesitated before replying :

" We live at an hotel, and I have not been accustomed to receiving calls from gentlemen."

Jack was politely urgent.

" Perhaps you would make an exception in my
case ?"

" My father does not approve of it."

Jack was desperate.

" I had hoped to be able to obtain your consent
and to say at the time of my call what I must say
now."

He dropped his voice so that it could be heard
by none but Lucy.

" I have something which should be in your
hands, which I think you will regard as of the
greatest value."

Lucy bent her dark eyes upon him most earnestly,
and Jack thought he saw in them a fleeting expression of alarm.

" Indeed ! "

" Yes.   A package of letters."

The color quickly rose to her cheeks and over-
spread them.

" A package of letters?   Of mine ? "

" I presume so."   Then dropping his voice still
lower: " They were in the possession of Cyril
Renfrew."

The color left her face so quickly that Jack
thought she was about to faint, and he cursed his
brutality.

But with a revulsion the color swept up deeper
than before.

" How came they—Call on me at two to-morrow
afternoon at the B——."

At this moment Dr. Sherman turned and offered
his arm to his daughter.   Noticing the heightened
color of Lucy's face, he looked at Jack scrutiniz-
ingly and not without kindly amusement.   That
unabashed young man bore the scrutiny well.

The lawyer and Jack bowed, and Dr. Sherman with his daughter on his arm walked away.

" That young gentleman evidently has a dangerous tongue," said Dr. Sherman to Lucy. " Beware of him, and do not show your excitement ·over compliments, however pleasing. Still you deserve them to-night, for you are looking very handsome."

Jack remained standing a moment where they left him. Then he said ·

" That trip is indefinitely postponed."

The principal attraction having withdrawn, Jack thought he would follow, escaping unobserved if possible.

This he did successfully. He had no fancy to go elsewhere. Within himself he possessed the food for interest and thought. So he went straightway to his own apartments.

Here he found his man Crimmins busily packing his trunks, in preparation for an early departure the next morning.

" You may stop that," said Jack.

" Sir."

" Yes, I am not going to-morrow. Something has occurred to-night to prevent me."

The obedient Crimmins began to unpack, and Jack, having donned his " blazer," lit a cigar, took an easy-chair, and soon sank into a profound reverie.

CHAPTER XIII.

AN INTERVIEW OF CONSEQUENCE.

IT may well be imagined that Lucy returned home in no enviable frame of mind. Her father, who had been greatly pleased with the entertainment, chatted quite gayly and compared it with the social festivities of his youth, both in New York and abroad. Indeed, he seemed to be seized with an unusual fit of garrulity, and after their arrival at home detained her with a long account of some ball of twenty years previous, to which Lucy gave only outward heed, so anxious was she to get to her room, where she might seriously consider the effect the information she had that night received so singularly, might have upon her fortunes. When she was at length released she dismissed her maid from attendance upon her.

What alarmed her most was that the secret was in danger of becoming widespread. The thought that her secret was confined to herself, now that Renfrew was dead, had comforted her. She had feared that the detective had become possessed of it, and that thought had for a time frightened her, but upon that point she had been assured, and she was beginning to believe that the actor had after all destroyed the letters; but now she learned that they were in the hands of a fashionable young man. By what means? What use would he make of that information? And the secret they contained, with how many had he shared it? Indeed, her situation seemed to be worse than before. So long as Renfrew was alive and possessed it alone she had been enabled to keep it down by payments of money. Now it was quite likely to become the gossip of the clubs and the street. Surely it would reach the ears of Dr. Sherman ! She wished she had killed herself that night, as she had intended. To live in this fear and constant dread of exposure was worse than death. Yet she could not do it now. The hope she had entertained that she was wholly relieved, had brought with it a revulsion which made the act impossible. This she fully realized. She even wondered now how she could have contemplated it, and whether she really ever intended to do it, so far off did it seem.

Thus she thought and thought without seeing light, until the breaking of the gray dawn admonished her that she must at least make a pretense of resting. She did not believe she could sleep. But she was far more exhausted by the excitement she had undergone than she was conscious of, and soon fell into profound slumber.

It was only when aroused by her maid that she awoke and had barely time to prepare for breakfast, which she hurriedly did. Her first thought was of Jack and his call. She was exceedingly anxious to meet him and know the worst in store for her. Her second was how she could secure an uninterrupted interview with him, since her father never left their apartments until after lunch, and often remained in all the afternoon. Of course she could receive Mr. Gordon in one of the public parlors, but her continued absence from their own would attract the attention of Dr. Sherman, who was something of a martinet in his family. Besides there was danger that when Jack's card was presented it would be before the Doctor, when, of course, he would have to be received in their own apartments, and with the presence of the Doctor the call would come to naught.

However, when breakfast was finished the Doctor smoothed away all difficulties by announcing that he was going out of town a short distance: and would not be back before the dinner-hour. This was a decided luxury, for she was thus free to manifest her impatience and show her anxiety unrestrained by fear of a pair of watchful eyes.

She spent a large portion of the morning in speculating upon the sort of person this Mr. Gordon might be. She had been rather impressed by his appearance and manner before he had presented himself in the formidable shape he had, as the possessor of her letters the night previous, and she was more than once on the point of donning her garments for the street and seeking some information of him, but was restrained by the unfounded fear that he might call in her absence.

Shortly after twelve, a caller, in the person of her chaperon, the pretty Mrs. Van Huyu, was ushered in. Here was the opportunity she so much desired, and she greeted her friend effusively.

" My dear," said that lady, " I ran around to see how you sustained the fatigues of last evening. Your father said you were not well."

" Nor have I been, for a day or two," replied Lucy. " But it was a mere nothing—I feel no ill effects from last night's dissipation."

" Then you came off better than I did," said the visitor, " for I find myself feverish, restless, nervous, and am tired of my own company. You do look well this morning, and were charming last night. I was proud of my charge and was fairly besieged for introductions."

Lucy laughed, but said nothing.

" My charge ! " continued the lady. " The idea ! You are as old as I am. To think only five years ago we were schoolmates, and now I am a married woman acting as your chaperon.   It is quite ridiculous."

"Who was that Mr. Gordon you brought to me?"

"I expected that question.   Indeed, I think the reason of my coming here this morning was to answer it."

"I am not so anxious to know that you needed to have come for that alone," replied Lucy with indifference, though it was a little white fib, for she was bursting with impatience.

"No, I presume not.   Yet in your heart you ought to be grateful to me.   You know you are just dying to have the answer."

"If I am, I am likely to die before I get it."

"Oh, the impatience of the dear thing !   Ah, I saw he succeeded in making himself very agreeable. · Do you think I was not observant of the parting?"

Lucy's color rose as she laughed.

"Why," said her visitor, noting it, "it is farther gone than I supposed.   But I'll not torture you. Mr. Gordon is regarded in many respects as the most eligible *parti* in the city.   Rich, well educated, more brains than usually falls to the lot of the *jeunesse doré*, not too far gone in dissipation, witty, good tempered, of good family, unburdened by father or mother, brother or sister.   Lacks something in good looks, but makes it up in distinction.   And, finally, is one of ' Mama Jamieson's ' young men—chief among the rest—*facile princeps*— you see I haven't forgotten Miss Waltham and my Latin."

"But is he a gentleman?"

"Is he not rich and well educated—well-born?"

"But he may not be a gentleman for all that."

"Oh, well, Jack Gordon *is* a gentleman. A kindly, big-hearted fellow, who would any time do one a kindness rather than an injury."

"I am glad to know that."

"Of course," said the lady, with a nervous little laugh which struck oddly on Lucy. "He ought to be much obliged to me, for I have done all in my power to assist him. I owe him several good turns, and when I see him I will sound your praises to him. I shall be the directing angel of this romance."

"Better wait until you see whether there is to be one."

"Oh, I am satisfied it is already begun. Well, Lucy dear, he is a dear, good boy. If I were in trouble I do not know any one I would rather put my trust in than Jack Gordon. He is true as steel."

"Who were the two young ladies with whom he seemed to be on such good terms?"

"Jealous indeed! Have no fear. They were Mollie Lowell and Lou Appleby—two dashing young ladies inclined to assume airs too loud and too fast to suit Jack's refined taste in women—well enough to flirt and chaff with, which he does to his heart's content, and as half—no, nine-tenths—of the young men do. It ends there."

Lucy had now learned all she could expect to, and she began to wish her visitor would depart. But to depart was far from Mrs. Van Huyn's purpose. She wanted company, and she frankly announced that she meant to lunch with her friend.

As the hour of two approached Lucy became so nervous as to betray her anxiety. So when Gordon's card was presented Mrs. Van Huyn laughed heartily.

"So this accounts for your anxiety. An appointment already. He loses no time in following up his advantage of last night. Come, shall I

dance at your wedding before the winter is over?
But why should I desire your marriage? The
estate is not such a happy one. Yet warnings are
of no use. Run down to him, my dear. Don't
mind me, I shall go at once."

They descended the stairs together, and parted
at the parlor door.

In the mean time Jack had been occupying the
time while waiting for Lucy's appearance in wondering how she would receive him. He feared she
would resent his interference in her affairs, for
after all it was impertinent officiousness on his
part.

When she entered he was, in fact, surprised at
her greeting. She was neither cold, haughty, nor
disdainful. On the contrary, there seemed to be
something appealing in the glance she cast upon
him, as if she were throwing herself upon his
mercy. Jack thought, "If she is charming at
night, she is irresistible in the morning."

As soon as they were seated he took from his
pocket the package of letters he had obtained from
Renfrew, and was about to speak, when a man who
had strolled into the parlor passed so close that
Jack waited for him to go by, which he did slowly,
posting himself in front of the mirror at the other
end of the room.

"This," he said, when the man was out of hearing,
"I am convinced belongs to you. I do not suppose so because I know its contents. I have never
read the letters, have never opened the package.
I know absolutely nothing of the nature of their
contents. I wish you to believe this—upon the
honor of a gentleman."

He handed them to her, conscious at the time of
the singularity of his endeavor to obtain the esteem
of one he believed to be the murderer of the
actor.

Lucy showed her surprise, and a glad look spread over her face. She observed the expression of earnestness on his, and believed him. She said so.

"I can not imagine how they came into your hands, Mr. Gordon," she added.

The man at the glass strolled back again, and so close that Jack, believing it to be intentional, glared at the man in so unmistakably a belligerent manner that he left the room, though during the whole conversation Jack could see he paced up and down the corridor.

Replying to Lucy he said :

"The story is a singular one, and perhaps would not be believed in its entirety. While I am glad I have been the means of restoring them to you, I can not say I am proud of the exploit."

Lucy looked at him, puzzled. After a moment's hesitation she said :

"You know, of course, that Mr. Renfrew is dead ?"

"Yes. Killed in his room night before last."

"Yes. I read the account in the papers."

Now it was Gordon's turn to be puzzled. He looked at the face of the girl. There was no blanching, not a quiver of trepidation, not an indication of agitation or remorse.

"She is an extraordinary woman," said Gordon to himself, partly in admiration and partly in amazement.

"I confess, Mr. Gordon," she continued, "you have performed a service for me, the value of which you can not realize. You can not know the gratitude I bear you for the favor and the generous way in which you have performed it."

Jack bowed, murmuring that he was only too glad to have been of real service to her.

"I would like to say something," continued Lucy, "and I hardly know how to say it."

She was evidently greatly embarrassed. The color was coming and going rapidly.

"If it embarrasses you," said Jack kindly, "leave it unsaid."

"No. I must say it in defense of myself," she persisted. "I hope you will try to understand me, and will believe me as earnestly as I do you."

Jack was sure he would.

"I read yesterday that Mr. Renfrew's reputation was not good ; that he was in the habit of inveigling young girls into letter-writing and then using that correspondence to his own—a very base— advantage."

Jack had heard that he had been given to *chantage.*

"I earnestly hope you will not believe this to be one of those cases ?"

This was a little more than Jack could believe when he remembered the conversation he had overheard. Fortunately for his politeness Lucy did not look up at him.

"There never was," she went on, "anything resembling a love episode between Mr. Renfrew and myself—not even the slightest form of flirtation."

The blushes were added to her cheek as she said this, and Jack was astonished to find how glad he was to hear her words.

"No," she continued, "I was not one of those silly girls who saw a hero in Mr. Renfrew. It is this I want you to believe."

Jack did believe then, because, having said what she had found it so hard to say, she bent her dark eyes upon him, and he had to believe in spite of himself.

"I shall not attempt to conceal from you," she went on after a moment's hesitation, "that this package contains letters written by me to Mr. Renfrew, but they are not love-letters. They were

written during a period of three years, and relate
to a matter which does not even remotely involve
the affections.   They relate to a fault committed
by me when I was a mere unsophisticated, irrespon-
sible school-girl—a fault which would be, if committed now at my age, a crime—a fault, the consequences of which have attended me since, and
from which I can not escape.   The knowledge of
this came into the possession of Mr. Renfrew five
years ago, and he has made me suffer bitterly for
the past three years."

"And he has paid the penalty at your hands,"
thought Jack, not without some sympathy.   Aloud
he said, "He is dead now, and you are free from
him."

"Yes, poor fellow.   His end was a terrible one."

Jack stared at her.   "By Jove!" he thought,
"you are a cool one, indeed."   Then aloud :

"You are not likely to be troubled again, if the
possession of those letters can secure you against
such trouble."

"I do not know through how many hands they
have passed," she replied.   "All may not have
treated them with the same delicacy and honor.
I do not know how they came into your hands."

"I received them direct from Mr. Cyril Renfrew."

"You received them from Ja—from Cyril?"

"Yes."

"I can hardly comprehend that.   Were you an
intimate friend of Mr. Renfrew?"

"I had never spoken to him half an hour before
he gave me that package."

Lucy looked at him in amazement.

"I can not understand it.   Did he give them to
you by mistake?   Ah," she said, a light breaking
in upon her, "he intended you should give them
to Dr. Sherman?"

"No, Dr. Sherman was not mentioned between

us. I demanded them from him—compelled him
to yield them up to me."

Lucy's face expressed utter bewilderment.

"I do not wonder you are puzzled, Miss Sherman," said Jack, smiling. "The case is almost
incredible in its details. You will pardon me, I
hope, if I do not recite it at length. That I should
have demanded the yielding up of the letters of a
lady of whose very name I was ignorant, is almost
impossible of belief, I understand, yet such is the
case. I had seen you without knowing who you
were. It had come to my knowledge that Renfrew possessed a package—of what I knew not—
but I did know its possession enabled him to hold
a power over you. I know it is inconceivable that
I should go to that man and demand its delivery to
me, trusting to my energy and sagacity to discover
you and deliver it to you. But such is the case."

Jack thought that this statement would be received with incredulity, and he looked into her face
with a deprecatory grimace, expecting to see such
an expression. He did not see it, but he saw a
variety of fleeting ones, none of which he could fix,
and he thought he saw a slight shudder quickly
suppressed. He rather expected to be laughed at,
but he would have been astounded if he could have
read her thoughts, for a suspicion had found lodg-
ment in her brain, that this man had killed her
persecutor. His unsatisfactory statement of an
act which certainly was incredible, and his evident
intention to suppress a part of the story, gave birth
to this suspicion.

Jack had intended to tell the cab story, but the
longer he talked with her—the longer he was
within the circle of her personal influence—the
more difficult he found the confession that he had
made her the subject of a bet—and such a bet—
that he had driven her in disguise, and listened to

a conversation which he had no business to hear. Feeling that he had not made the best impression in his last speech, for she seemed to freeze into stiffness, he tried to correct it.

" Perhaps some time when we know each other better, I can tell you how that knowledge came to me. When you know me better, then, what now you might call my impertinence would be con- doued—when I could tell you how I came to offi- ciously intermeddle in your affairs, and why, when it would not then take on the appearance of offense, it might now."

He had not improved affairs. Lucy was only the more confirmed in her suspicions that he had quarreled with Renfrew and killed him.

Jack was smiling, rather enjoying her air of be- wilderment.

" But of this you can rest assured," continued Jack, since she did not speak. " If you are satis- fied that no one, other than Renfrew, possessed your secret, you are perfectly safe. The package went from his keeping into mine, and I restore it to you just as I received it."

" He is a gentleman, anyhow," thought Lucy.

" Yes," he repeated, " just as I received it, and I am as ignorant of its contents as when I went to see him."

" When you went to see him ? " she repeated. " When was that ? "

" The day of his murder—in the afternoon."

" Oh, I went to see him that day too."

" Miss Sherman," said Jack earnestly, " three people called to see Renfrew that afternoon. One of them killed the actor. Two of them are here now talking with each other. The knowledge that we called is confined to ourselves. Let me advise you—let me urge you to keep that knowledge to yourself. I shall do the same. If we do not we shall be involved, at least as witnesses, at the examination. In your case you might be compelled to disclose your secret, and, possibly, whether or not you returned for a second visit. But," and he spoke most impressively, " burn that package. Put it out of your power to produce it again."

Lucy was about to say something as to her visit, when Jack cautioned her to burn the letters, and diverted her attention to its necessity.

Jack had risen with his remark, and had seen the warm blood sweep up over Lucy's cheek as he had so impressively warned her.

" Yes," he said, with a pang at his heart, "she caused the death of Renfrew."

" Yes," she said, as she considered the earnestness of Jack's warning and misapprehended it, " he surely killed Jacob."

They shook hands, and as they parted, the man who had hovered about the door came down the corridor.

Jack walked along the street in a singular frame of mind.

" Now, by Jove ! here is a fine condition of things for an amiable and respectable, not to say a talented and highly virtuous young man. Here am I in collusion with a young lady who has a mysterious epoch in her life, from the consequences of which she escapes by calmly suspending the breath of the wretch who knows all about the epoch and can injure her. And what is worse, the more I see her the more fascinated I am with her."

He strode along in profound thought for a while. Then he said aloud :

" Hang it all ! I'll keep her secret, no matter what the consequences. To the devil with prudence !"

Lucy hastened to her own room, and locking the door opened the package. From it fell a long paper neatly folded.   She found it to be a succinct statement of the fault—the crime—she had referred to in her conversation with Gordon.   This made her angry, for she saw in it proof of the intention of Renfrew to expose her.

She hastily examined the letters and found that all she had written were there—not one missing ; but she found another also which was not written by her.   Yet the hand seemed familiar to her, though she could not determine it, however hard she tried.   It was signed " Dollie Dux."   She folded it up and laid it away in her desk.   Her own she threw into the fire one by one and saw them burn with satisfaction.

" There ! " she said, as the last one turned black and shriveled up.   " There is the last bit of evidence against me.   Get it who can.   Jacob is dead, and if he has told no one, and it is not likely he has, the secret is mine alone.   Mr. Gordon says he does not know, and I believe him."

She drew up a small easy-chair before the grate, and nestling in its soft cushions gave herself up to thoughts of Gordon.

How came he to interfere ?   And why ?   Beyond this she could not get.   Strive she ever so hard she could not get a bit of ground to stand upon from which to reason.

Was he responsible for Renfrew's death ?   She tried hard to believe the contrary; but if his guarded words did not justify that suspicion, what did they mean ?   She was afraid he had—that he had quarreled with the actor she was certain, perhaps over her own letters, and then in a moment of anger had done the fearful deed.   Men did such things when they were exasperated ; even gentlemen.   She had read of such cases.

At all events he had done her great service—a very great service—for he had removed her entirely from danger. She ought to be grateful to him, and she was. Had he not saved her from exposure and ruin? He had been true to her and she should be to him—true as steel. Not a word should fall from her that would injure him, notwithstanding he had done this deed. She owed him far too much. He could depend on her, no matter what he had done.

Then she thought of her attempt to recover her letters from Captain Lawton. She thought now it was a mistake, and she had promised to go again in a week. But there was no need. She would write him that her letters had been recovered, and therefore would not call again.

Acting upon the impulse, she wrote to the Captain, taking care not to sign any name, but indicating who the writer was by this sentence : " You will recollect I called upon you yesterday with reference to letters signed by ' Lucy,' presuming then they were in the possession of the late Cyril Renfrew."

When the Captain received it he laughed long and heartily, and called for a report of one of his aids. " You need not shadow her any longer," he said. " Devote yourself to Mr. John Gordon."

CHAPTER XIV.

SETTING THE LINES.

THE days moved on and Captain Lawton found himself but little nearer the end of his search than he was on the night of the murder. He still adhered to the theory that a woman had committed the deed, and one who had been goaded by Renfrew into desperation. But there he stopped, and neither could his superior officer, who agreed with him as to the theory, suggest a line of policy which, if followed, promised results of the kind desired. The chief obstacle to progress was found in the secretive life and methods of the dead actor. . He was apparently a man without family or relations. Certainly he was without intimates or confidants. He had succeeded in tracing Renfrew back to the day he first appeared at a theater as an applicant for employment. An old prompter said to the Captain :

"I recollect well the day he appeared. Sidewing, the stage-manager, and I were looking over the supernumeraries one day after a rehearsal, and thinking we wanted a leader who could speak a line or two, when a good-looking young fellow came in and, leaning over the rail of the orchestra, said : ' I have called to see if you would give me a chance.' I said to Sidewing, ' He looks it well enough.' Said Sidewing, ' What experience have you had ?' ' None whatever,' he replied. Sidewing shook his head, but I said, ' Give him a trial ; bring him up and give him a rehearsal.' So Sidewing did. He was so intelligent and quick that he got the speeches in twenty minutes just as Sidewing wanted them, and he rehearsed next day satisfactorily with the 'supes.' He was engaged. We kept on giving him little speaking parts, and so he grew. That was his beginning. Nobody ever knew where he came from."

From all the Captain could hear, Renfrew never had made a confidant of any one and never associated with his fellows of the stage. No one, therefore, could help trace any of the correspondents whose letters indicated close intimacy with him. A few were, but it was soon apparent that they had gone but a little way with him and could tell nothing. The rank of life of his correspondents helped to prevent discovery. The coroner's inquest had elicited nothing whatever, and the Inspector said to the Captain one day : " It is going to be an addition to the list of mysterious murders."

The Captain remarked in the same conversation, " Of course, we know that Miss Sherman called upon him on the day of the murder. But she was the first one. I have settled that conclusively. So far we have been unable to discover the other two. Of course the third one is the real one. The second might assist us. I am quite certain, and I believe you agree with me, that Miss Sherman had no connection with those who followed."

" Yes," replied his superior officer. " I agree with you entirely in that. That girl is too frank and confiding to have the burden of that murder on her soul."

" I have gone over Oliver's work again," continued the Captain, " and there is not a pistol in town to compare with the one found."

" I can not criticise your work, Captain," said his superior, " except in one particular. It doesn't seem to me that you have done all you could to discover what Miss Sherman knows about Renfrew and his surroundings. Why don't you see her again; perhaps by gaining her confidence you might obtain something from her."

" I think I sounded her pretty exhaustively when she came to see me," replied the Captain. " I don't think she knows anything. But I'll try. There is one thing, however, that I ought to discover and I will. You remember that Fagan, who was shadowing her, reported that young Gordon called upon her and delivered to her a package. You recollect that she wrote me the same day that she had recovered her letters. I received her note a week ago to-day. Now the package Gordon gave her was evidently the letters she wanted to recover. How did Gordon get them ? And from whom ? From Renfrew ? If so, when ? These inquiries ought to be made."

" You are right," rejoined the Inspector. " What relation does Gordon bear to her ? "

" I don't know. I have supposed him to be a beau of hers. They move in the same circle."

" Well, follow it up. Perhaps you ought to have done so before."

" Nothing is lost. I have had them both shadowed, and there were other things to be done while the trail was fresh."

" Well, lose no time now," said the Inspector, putting an end to the interview.

During the week following the delivery of the package to her, Lucy had experienced a greater ease of mind than she had enjoyed for three years previously. The dreadful contingency which was always present had disappeared in the death of Renfrew and the recovery and burning of her letters. She felt like one who had escaped from a prison, or rather like one who had been released. She was free—there was no dreadful reckoning time drawing day by day closer. There was no fear at night that she would awaken to a new demand in the morning ; there was no longer a sickening recollection on awaking that a sum of money must be collected before night or she would be ruined. Gladness filled her heart and left no room for the remorse which had previously made her regard her fault—her crime—as something wretched and horrible. Indeed, she began to think that the trespass was, after all, a small thing, not worth the sorrow and regret she had wasted upon it. She did not stop to think that the remorse was quite as much a strong regret that by reason of the fault—the crime—she had put herself in the power of Renfrew, and was not sorrow for the crime itself. She was in these days so bright and gladsome that Dr. Sherman congratulated her upon her return to health, and said that in recovering it she had renewed the lightheartedness of girlhood.

During this week, too, she saw a great deal of Jack Gordon. If it was not at Mrs. Van Huyn's, it was at Mrs. Jamieson's, and if not there, Jack found his way to the hotel. It was singular, she had remarked to herself, how he seemed to run across her path at all sorts of odd hours. Two weeks previously she had not known him or even seen him. Now, she could not make a call that he did not drop in at the same place. Indeed she could hardly go to shop anywhere that she did not meet him. This gave her a good deal to think about, or, perhaps it were better said, it gave her reason to think a great deal about Jack. She did, and the more she saw him the better she liked him. She admitted this to herself with a blush.

On Jack's part he frankly confessed to himself that the girl fascinated him. He was far from admitting he was in love with her or anything approaching it. Her beauty, the brightness of her

mind, the virility of her individuality, he acknowledged strongly attracted him ; and moreover she
was a study of interest, knowing as he did that she
was what she was.   Of all the contradictory persons he had ever met, she puzzled him most, and
he thought that it must be the peculiarity of her
moral   nature,   so   perverted   and   distorted,   that
caused   the   fascination.   Having   delivered   her
letters, there was no   reason why he   should not
have carried into effect his prudent determination
to leave the city.   But he could not.   He could
not bring himself to consent to an interruption of
the acquaintance which had been formed.   Indeed,
he had gotten into that condition when he considered that day ill spent a portion of which was
not passed in her society.   "Now," said he to himself one day, rather proudly and self-approvingly,
"most men in my shoes would have fallen des-
perately in love with her.   But I only find in her
an interest of an intense and fascinating kind, like
that I had in that curious and beautiful snake I
used to go to see in the Park daily a couple of
years ago.   The idea of loving one who is given
to the pleasant pursuit of assassination !   She is
beautiful, and it is true that one side of her nature
is very sweet and winsome."

Ah, Jack !

The Captain lost no time in acting on his superior's command.   Dressing himself with more
than usual care, he shortly presented himself at
the desk of the B—— hotel and desired his card to
be sent to Miss Sherman.

Fortunately for that young lády, she was in the
corridor near the parlor when the Captain's card
was brought to her by an attendant.

Not seriously alarmed, but much perplexed, she
hastened to the public parlor where the detective
was awaiting her.

As she entered he arose and greeted her by name.

"You know my name?" she inquired.

"Yes," he replied smilingly, "or I should not have been able to send my card to you."

"But I thought I had taken all precautions to prevent your knowing it."

"To learn the name of any one in the city is a very simple matter for the police department," he replied blandly. "I have known your name since the day you called upon me."

Lucy was dumbfounded; she had no reply she could make. The Captain continued:

"I received your note. I am glad you recovered your letters. You must feel easier. I suppose you have burned them?"

"Yes," she replied wonderingly.

"That was wise. They are now out of the way forever."

He was striving to gain her confidence, but Lucy felt that his call upon her was not made simply to felicitate her upon her recovery of her letters, and this thought alarmed her.

"Through what means did you regain them?" he asked, as if he was inspired by an interest in her fortunes.

She had apprehended that question and dreaded it.·

"I can not tell you that," she replied hurriedly.

The Captain smiled. It was his habit to smile when he was rebuffed, and it was a smile which meant that he was put off for the present, but he would get round to it again soon.

"I think I can convince you in a moment that it would be wise to do so?"

"No, I can't do it and I won't."

"Of course I have no desire to force you to do anything against your will."

Lucy drew herself up with resentment and said:

"Your desires can not influence me in any way."
The Captain smiled and continued :

"I would respectfully call your attention to the
fact that justice must be done.   You see I've got
to make a report some time or another on this case,
and I've got to tell everything that might seem to
bear on it—even of your call on me.   Now, it
wouldn't be pleasant, would it, to have your name
dragged in ?   Suppose then you were to make a
clean breast of it to me, I could judge whether it
was necessary to say anything about it.   If I do
have to put your name in the report as one who
knows something that might be important, why,
you see, you might have to go on the witness
stand and have to answer questions as to your
relations to Renfrew, you know."

Lucy was frightened ; all the horrible possibilities rolled in upon her, and the Captain, seeing the
impression he had made, followed up his advantage :

"I haven't got anything I want to conceal from
you.   I don't think for a moment that there is anything you want to hide for yourself except about
the letters and your connection with Renfrew.
You don't want to get dragged into this affair,
nor do you want any friend of yours dragged in.
I know how it is, and you think the way to keep
out is to keep your mouth shut.   Now that's where
you make a mistake.   I've got to find something
out about Renfrew, about his friends, his life, and
ways—"

"But I don't know anything about him or how he
lived.   I had just this foolish flirtation with him,"
interrupted Lucy, in her alarm and agitation cling-
ing to her first story.

This so entirely coincided with the Captain's
views that he remarked as he continued :

"If you say so, why of course I'll believe you.
That's what you said before, and what **you say** now,

So that ends that part, unless you will let me ask, if you knew any one who did know Renfrew?"

"No, I never did," replied Lucy promptly.

"That's what I expected," continued the Captain. " But then there's your recovery of your letters. How did that come about? If Renfrew gave those letters to any one, why, it must have been some one he was friendly to, intimate with, you know. Now, all I want to know is that man, so I could talk with him. See! That would let you out. Your name wouldn't come out because there wouldn't be any necessity."

"He could tell you nothing."

" Are you sure of that?"

" Quite. He told me so himself."

" Still, he might know something it would be of value for me to know?"

" I am quite sure it would be useless. He never saw Mr. Renfrew until the day of—"

She stopped short, for she was heedlessly rushing into a blunder. The Captain, who was gazing upon her with a bland, even a vacuous stare, never by so much as a quiver intimated that he saw anything unusual in her hesitation. But, he completed the sentence for her—" the murder—ah, the young man of whom we have no trace."

" No, the day before the delivery of the package to me."

Lucy thought she had cleverly recovered herself. Moreover, as she looked at the Captain, she thought, " These detectives have the reputation of being very clever, but if they are all like this one they are very stupid."

The " very stupid " detective confirmed her in her opinion by replying :

" If that is so, may be you are right. Let me see, you received that package Thursday of last week."

" How do you know that ? "

" That's the day you wrote me you had got them. The day before you were at my office looking for them."

Lucy for the first time saw how ill-advised the writing of that note was. She made no reply.

The Captain, taking a small memorandum-book from his vest-pocket, turned over the leaves deliberately, Lucy eyeing him suspiciously.

Finally he said :

" The gentleman you received it from was Mr. John Gordon."

Lucy was overwhelmed ; the Captain saw that he had made a hit.

" It was the package he gave you in this very room."

She was speechless, angry, frightened.

" If he talked with Renfrew the day before that, then it must have been on the day of the murder."

The reasoning was conclusive. He was not so stupid after all.

" If he saw Renfrew and talked to him on the day of the murder, then he must have seen the actor in his rooms, for Renfrew didn't leave 'em that day. So Mr. Gordon must have been the young man who called on him that we've been looking for and couldn't find."

She could not answer. The accuracy of his reasoning overpowered her.

" This makes it necessary to see Mr. Gordon," said the Captain, rising. " I thank you, lady, for your information. There's no necessity for your name to come into the report."

He bowed, walked away, leaving Lucy crushed and thoroughly alarmed.

Oh, what had she done ! By her heedlessness she had brought trouble on one who had only known her to befriend her. She had been watched.

They had both been spied upon. She must see Mr. Gordon and at once. She ran to her room and wrote a note briefly :

"DEAR MR. GORDON :—

"I must see you as soon as possible. Do come at once, please. Something terrible has occurred. It affects you.

"Very gratefully yours,

"LUCY SHERMAN."

But his address? She did not know it. She thought a moment, then hastily donning her outer garments, hurried to the house of her friend and chaperon, Mrs. Van Huyu, to obtain Jack's address, from whence she sent it. Then hurrying back, she awaited with anxiety his coming.

In the mean time Captain Lawton went back to the headquarters quite satisfied with his afternoon's work. "One more step forward," he said, " and we'll get to the third caller and the one."

CHAPTER XV.

JACK IS ENTANGLED.

IT so happened that on the day when Lucy sent so urgently for him, Jack had been induced to go up-town and look at some purchases of horses " Dizzy " Lowell had been making, and instead of returning to his apartments as was his invariable custom in the late afternoon, had dined with his friend, stayed the evening with him and " Dizzy's " fair sister, Mollie, until a late hour. Indeed, it was so late . when he did return and found the note and two subsequent ones Lucy had sent in her extreme urgency, that it was out of the question to think of calling upon her that night. He determined he would go to her as early the next morning as the proprieties would permit.

" I wonder what it is that disturbs the fair dispatcher of men ? " he said to himself, as he prepared to disrobe for the night. " It affects me, does it ? Well, it's all very flattering to have so beautiful a woman so anxious about your welfare, Jack, my boy, but—" his sentence ended in a yawn, and was never completed.

Earlier than usual the next morning Jack dressed and went to breakfast at the restaurant which he usually patronized.

Leisurely reading his paper and sipping his coffee, so as to consume as much time as possible, he was not aware that the person sitting at the table near by was patiently waiting for him to rise.

When he did, the person stepped across the room, and politely said :

" I presume I address Mr. Gordon—Mr. John Gordon ? "

" That is my name," replied Jack courteously, picking up his papers from the table.

" Captain Lawton wishes to see you."

The tone in which this was said rather nettled Jack, for it conveyed the idea that there was nothing left for him to do but to run at once to the Captain.

" Captain who ? " said Jack stiffly.

" Captain Lawton, the detective."

" Well, if Captain Lawton, the detective, wants to see me, let him come at any hour I am at home," said Jack, taking his hat from an adjoining chair.

" The business is important," was the reply.

" It must be to him then, for it is not to me. So much more reason why he should seek me. I do not desire to see Captain Lawton."

The messenger was embarrassed, and hesitated as if he did not know how to proceed.

Jack moved off as if to leave the room.

" It would be wiser if you were to call upon him."

" I never do wise things," retorted Jack. " So I won't go. Your friend the Captain is impertinent."

" I am afraid you don't understand," said the man, after a moment's hesitation. " You have no choice. My instructions were to treat you with every consideration. But you make it hard for me."

A light broke in on Jack.

" Who are you ? "

" Officer Oliver, of the detective force."

" Oh ! What does the Captain want of me ? "

" He will inform you when you see him."

" Very well, I will call upon him later in the day,

I have a matter to attend to which will occupy an hour."

"That I can not permit, sir. The Captain is waiting for you now."

By this time Jack recognized that he was practically under arrest. He was angry, but retained sufficient self-command to exercise his common-sense, and he realized it were better to yield than to make a scene.

"Very well, I will go," he said. "Follow. me at some distance."

Jack went out, followed by the detective, and took the street-car which passed the door. Having smothered his irritation as best he could, and having given himself up to cool thought, he found reasons to connect his summons to the Central Office with Lucy's urgent notes of the night previons. He believed that by some means he had been identified with the young man who had called on Renfrew on that fateful day, and he heartily condemned himself for not having left the town, as he promised himself to do, on the morning following the murder.

He was deep in thought when his attention was arrested by the detective, who, rising from his seat, cast a significant look on Jack. He saw that they were at the end of the journey by the street-car.

Alighting, he walked briskly to the Headquarters, followed by his attendant. As he entered he was directed to the office of the Captain.

"Good-morning, Mr. Gordon," said that official, rising and extending his hand, which Jack quietly ignored, and, instead, took a chair in a part of the room that suited him. The captain looked with some interest upon Jack's coolness, and, indeed, ostentatious insolence.

"I'm afraid," he began, "that my summons—"

"Your summons was a piece of impertinence,"

interrupted Jack, " to which I would not have submitted but that I did not want a scene. If you think I am going to submit tamely to this, you do not know me. I propose to punish you for this."

" You'll punish no one but yourself, Mr. Gordon," said the Captain, with his inscrutable smile.

Jack looked at the Captain straight in the eyes with the utmost contempt expressed on his countenance.

"You are made of too poor stuff to think of frightening me. I don't frighten. I am a very different kind of a person from the poor criminals you are in the habit of dealing with. I am your superior in the one thing in which you might expect to approach my level—shrewdness."

Jack was quite evidently endeavoring to irritate the Captain, hoping to get up a quarrel under the cover of which he could refuse to answer such questions as would involve the name of Lucy.

" Now go on," he continued, "and be quick about it. Yes, I called on Renfrew the day he was murdered. That is what you want to know?"

The Captain was somewhat disconcerted by this sudden admission, and felt that he had before him a more difficult case than he had bargained for. He had only known Gordon as one of the fashionable young men of the day, and had supposed he was one who could be easily frightened, if not because of the want of inherent manhood, at least through fear of being produced on the witness stand. He soon found that in this he was mistaken. He did conclude, however, Jack had adopted the tone he had for the purpose of irritating him.

" I regret," he said, " you take my summons—"

" Never mind your regrets," interrupted Jack, " I recognize that you detectives are necessary evils, and so long as there are men to be found low enough to follow spying as a business for money, we must be annoyed by them. Get on with your business."

Stung as he **was**, the Captain bravely curbed his temper.

" I sent for you," replied the Captain, firmly and decidedly,—" I sent for you to know from whom you received that package of letters you gave Miss Sherman on Friday last ? "

" You're too inquisitive," replied Jack ; but notwithstanding his self-possession he was disturbed. How did the Captain know the package had been delivered ? Had Lucy admitted it ? She must have done so. Evidently the detective knew Lucy had called on Renfrew the day of the murder. Yes, that was it. They had frightened her into an admission, as they were trying to frighten him. He must be wary and carefully guard every answer. The Captain discovered that he was not an easy subject.

" I can understand your annoyance, Mr. Gordon," replied the detective with great firmness. " But you must understand that there is nothing inquisitive in trying to trace crime. You are not wise in your treatment of me. Your insults do not prevent me from knowing that you got those letters from Cyril Renfrew."

" If you knew, why did you ask ? " hotly returned Jack. " That is another impertinence."

" You got those letters," continued the detective, ignoring Jack's remark, " on the day—on the afternoon of the day he was murdered."

" Well, and what then ? "

" You must see that brings you pretty close to the murder."

" No, I do not."

" It makes you a witness at the trial."

" Bah, you talk like a child ! "

"Why did he give them to you?"

Jack did not answer.

"He refused to give them to the one who wrote them an hour previous when she visited him," continned the Captain.

"He has evidently frightened Lucy into telling," thought Jack. "That was the reason of her urgent notes. Well, as she didn't know how I got them she couldn't tell him; that's why he sends for me."

"I am waiting for your answer, Mr. Gordon," said the detective, in the tone of one who was determined to have his question answered. "Why did he give them to you?"

"Because I asked for them."

"Did you go at the request of the lady?"

"No, I did not."

The Captain was not prepared for this answer, and it changed the course of his proposed examination.

"Then why did you go to him for those particular letters?"

"Now," said Jack, leaning forward and looking steadily at the detective, "let us understand each other. I know, and you know, that you have no more right to ask me questions than the first boy in the street. You detectives assume a right from your position, which is simply that of thief-taker. No compulsion rests upon me to answer you. I know that, and you know it. Guilty men who desire to placate you recognize your right,—I don't. You had no business to summon me here. The fact that I call on a man one day, and that subsequently, after others have called upon him, he is murdered, gives you no right over me. There is a power you do possess,—it is the same a mosquito has, the power to annoy--a power you use in the same way that scoundrel Renfrew did—it is a kind of blackmail. Having made you understand that I know just how we stand, and having nothing to conceal, I'll answer your question. It was because I knew that Renfrew had a package of letters from the lady which he was using to her disadvantage. I was interested in the lady, and I served her because I knew she was in trouble."   .

" She gave you her confidence then ? "

" How else do you suppose I knew it'? "

Jack had hesitated over this reply, and the detective promptly noted the hesitation without understanding it.

" I ask you the question,' he said.

" And I reply with another," retorted Jack.

The Captain thought he was not making much progress.

" Did Renfrew yield them up willingly ? "

" Yes, when he knew he had to, or stand the consequence of a prosecution for blackmail."

" But that would have ruined the lady," the Captain ventured.

" Possibly," said Jack, and then laughed. " He was the kind of fellow you took me for—easily frightened. But what is the use of all this ? Either you are purposely stupid, or you are unfit for your place if you can not see that the moment a man of determination stepped in between this fellow and the girl, his game was up. When she refused to be plundered longer, backed by a male friend, he couldn't expose her without subjecting himself to prosecution for blackmail. Just as soon as there was a third person in the case, he was done. He could succeed only through her fear and silence. After that it was easy to receive and demand the letters. He was already liable."

" This is a keen, able fellow," said the detective to himself. Then aloud: " What was the nature of those letters ? "

"I don't know."

"The lady never told you?"

"No."

"Yet you assisted her without knowing what they were about?"

"Precisely. It was enough to know that she was in trouble."

"Ah, a gallant gentleman—a generous friend," sneered the detective. He was trying to irritate Jack.

"As you say," replied Jack, smiling to think what the Captain would say if he knew all.

"How long was this package in your possession?"

"A couple of days."

"And you never read the letters?"

"No. They were secrets of the lady."

"Very remarkable. Now, I would have read those letters."

"Undoubtedly. But you see I am a gentleman, and a gentleman is hampered by considerations of honor and delicacy."

This was said with the most studied insolence. The Captain bit his lip to restrain the angry words that leaped to his tongue, all the more annoyed that he himself had made the opening for the shot.

"So Renfrew yielded willingly?" he pursued.

"Yes. After argument."

"Enforced by a bullet, and when he could not prevent it?" said the Captain maliciously.

Jack looked at him with contempt.

"You are silly. If you know I went to see Renfrew, you must know that a lady called to see him after I did."

"Still, she may have found him dead and gone away quietly."

"Pshaw," said Jack contemptuously, "this sort of sparring is useless! You know that the occupant of a neighboring room heard the two quarreling after I went away."

" Who was the lady who came after you ? "

"I don't know."

" What were your relations to her? "

" Don't try any traps with me. I've told you the truth. I don't know who she was."

". Was it Miss Sherman ? "

" When I tell you I don't know who she was, I tell you she was not Miss Sherman. That was plain to be seen. . Whoever it was, was shorter and more mature than Miss Sherman."

" What do you know about Renfrew? "

" Nothing. Never saw him before that day to talk to him."

" I believe the fellow," the Captain said to himself. " He is telling the truth, but there is something he is holding back."

He rose, and, going to his desk, opened a drawer from which he took some papers. As he did so, he made sure that Gordon was watching him.

He took out, the pistol with which Renfrew had been killed, and laid it in plain sight.

Gordon started on seeing it, and leaned forward to look at it. The detective followed the lead thus given him.

Lifting a paper from the drawer, he looked over it, literally, for his eyes were upon Gordon, and he saw a singular variety of expressions flit over Jack's face, the most marked of which were surprise and perplexity. Putting the paper back again in the drawer, he picked up the pistol, saying:

" This is the joker that did for Renfrew."

" This ? " said Jack in blank amazement. Then he stretched out his hand for it. The Captain passed it to him.

Jack looked at it most carefully ; examined it in every part ; and then, to the Captain's intense surprise, touched a concealed spring, revealing in the end of the butt a receptacle for caps—a feature of the pistol which no one had discovered before, and which argued an intimate acquaintance with it upon the part of Jack. The truth was Jack had betrayed himself. He had been attacked from a point where he expected none. He passed it back to the Captain without a word.

" Whose pistol is that ? " demanded the detective.

" I don't know," replied Jack. This time the hesitation was unmistakable.

" Now you are not telling me the truth," said the Captain. " You recognized it the moment you saw it, and I am going to find out whose it is."

" I suppose there are more than one of this kind made," said Jack uneasily.

This was almost a confession. The fact was, Jack was overwhelmed with astonishment.

" True," said the detective, " but its mate can't be found in this city. Now, whose is it ? "

Jack was conscious of his error, and he did not reply.

" Does this pistol belong to Miss Lucy Sherman ? "

" I never saw it or one like it in her possession or of any one belonging to her." He had recovered possession of himself.

" Then if it does not belong to her, who does it belong to ? "

Jack saw that he could not make it plain that it was not Lucy's without going further than he intended to. He did not reply.

" Whose pistol do you think that is ? " demanded the Captain again.

" I won't tell you," replied Jack; and then determining to save Lucy, he added : " I think I have seen a similar pistol in the possession of a person who has not yet been mentioned, even remotely, in this matter; but I am going to make no mistake, and will throw suspicion on nobody until I am certain."

" Ah ! Then we've got to the point when I shall not handle you with gloves any longer."

" Pouf ! "

" Do you know the conclusions you force me to?"

" No, nor do I care."

'' Either you recognize that pistol as your own, or you have seen that particular pistol in the possession of some else."

" Well, what then ? "

" You are connected with that murder."

" And then what ? "

" You are either the murderer or the one witness who can point directly to the person who did the deed."

" And then what ? "

" Well, for the present, you have lost your liberty."

Jack was hardly prepared for this statement, but he was unmoved.

" As for being the murderer, you know that is absurd. As for telling you who I think may have owned that pistol, or guessing at it, that is still more absurd," he replied.

" All right, you will stay here until I return."

He touched an electric button on his desk twice. Two men entered.

" Search this man for arms," he continued.

Jack laughed contemptuously.

" I have none," he said, " but look for them."

None having been found, the Captain took his hat and coat, saying to the two officers who had come at his bidding :

"Watch this man until I come back. I am going to consult the Inspector."

Jack laughed again, and asked for a newspaper.

CHAPTER XVI.

BEHIND THE BARS.

LUCY awaited with impatience almost unbear-
able the coming of Jack in response to her
urgent letters. When it grew too late to expect him that night, she retired worried, and in no
enviable frame of mind.

The next morning, having waited a reasonable
time and unable to bear the suspense longer, she
ordered her carriage and accompanied by her faithful maid drove to Gordon's apartments. Fortunately for her, Dr. Sherman had left the city for a
few days, and she was comparatively a free agent.

Arriving at the house where Gordon lived, she
sent her maid for the janitor, who said Mr. Gordon had gone out early in the morning, and he was
quite certain had not returned. However, he would
go to his rooms and find out. After a few minutes he
returned accompanied by Crimmins, who evidently
was quite agitated. He said that Mr. Gordon had
been absent all the day previous, not returning
until after midnight ; that it was not until then that
he had read the three letters awaiting him : that
he seemed much annoyed, and was disposed to
blame Crimmins for not hunting him up to deliver
them ; that that morning he had gone out to breakfast, saying he would be away two hours ; he had
seen nothing of him since, but he had just then received a note from Mr. Gordon telling him to bring
a lot of clothing and reading-material to the Ludlow Street Jail.

Lucy, now thoroughly alarmed, was quite certain he was imprisoned as a result of her want of caution in her interview with Captain Lawton. It was to prevent just this that she had so urgently written him the night previous, and all her efforts had been unavailing. She must see him, and she must tell him that it was not because she had not intended to be true to him that he was now in this trouble.

She gave orders to be driven to the Central Office. Being ushered into the presence of the Captain, she found that official somewhat ruffled, and not feeling kindly toward Jack, for that young gentleman had not only not treated him with deference, but had shown him positive contempt. He received the lady politely, however.

"I have called to know where Mr. Gordon is," said Lucy, scorning all subterfuge. "Do you know where he is?"

The Captain smiled.

"Yes, I think I know something of his whereabouts."

"Oh, then, please tell me."

"May I ask what your relations to Mr. Gordon are?"

"He is a very dear friend."

The Captain smiled again, and not unkindly, for he thought they were lovers, and is it not said that 'all the world loves a lover'? But if the detective could have known that these two young people were not acquainted two weeks previous to that day, he would have had other food for thought. But how was he to know? There was every indication of a long, intimate, and confidential acquaintance.

"But where is he?" she asked imploringly.

"He is detained as an important witness in the Renfrew case."

Lucy gave a gasp which was indicative both of

the confirmation of her fears and of her relief in finding he was not arrested for murder, but she was greatly distressed.

" I want to see him," she said. " I must see him."

The Captain thought a moment. His impulse was to send for Jack and let him meet Lucy in his presence. Then he doubted whether their conversation would be unrestrained enough to be of value to him. Perhaps it would be better to let them meet at the jail, where he might overhear their conversation. So he said :

" I will see whether it is possible. Wait here a moment."

Going into the outer room he called an officer in waiting, and instructed him to go to the place where Gordon was confined and say to the warden that in a short time a lady would call asking to see him ; that he, the Captain, wanted her to see Gordon, but not until after he had had time to get to the jail after her.

Then he went back to Lucy.

" I have arranged so that you can see Mr. Gordon presently," he said. " But I should like to ask you a question before you go."

Lucy was impatient to be off, and made no effort to conceal her feelings. To this the Captain gave no heed ; he was seeking to gain time for his messenger to get to the jail.

" I should like to know," he asked, " exactly what the relations were between you and Renfrew ? "

Lucy, however, had had quite enough of Captain Lawton's questions. Was not Jack now imprisoned through her answers ? She had grown wise and prudent. The Captain might question and question, but he would have nothing more from her.

" I have nothing more to tell you than I have already told you."

" Does that mean," he asked, with that inserut-
able smile of his, " that you have nothing more to
tell me, or that you will not tell me any more?"

" Both."

The Captain smiled again.

" Can you not even tell me how long ago it **was**
that you confided the story of your trouble to Mr.
Gordon ? "·

An expression of obstinacy had settled on
Lucy's face, and this inquiry, which was a shot
even nearer home than the detective himself imagined, she would not respond to, but only because
she had made up her mind not to answer at all.

The Captain noted her obstinacy, but he amused
himself.

" Are you not afraid of becoming mixed up in a
scandal by refusing to tell ? "

" I don't care about a scandal—I don't care
anything about a scandal.   I want to see Mr. Gordon.   That's all."

" Oh, very well," laughed the detective.   " You
will find Mr. Gordon at the Ludlow Street Jail.
You have but to inquire for him."

He bowed her out, and prepared to follow
her.

The doors flew open at her approach and she
was received with politeness.   But she waited
some time before Jack was brought to her.   He
was greatly surprised to find his visitor was Lucy,
but nevertheless very glad to see ber.

Lucy, running impulsively to him, said :

" Oh, Mr. Gordon, this is all my fault.   You are
in trouble—in this disgraceful place—all through
me."

" Hush !" said Gordon.   " Compose yourself and
be careful what you say.   We may be overheard."

They were, though Jack did not know it.

" Do not think it is your fault.   There is no

danger in my situation—there is only some tempo. rary inconvenience."

" No danger," she repeated, looking at him anxiously, while the tears came into her eyes at the thought.

Jack saw the tears and was touched. He led her to a corner where there were two chairs, near a window looking out on a dead wall, and, seating her in one, took the other.

" Your sympathy, Miss Sherman, is very grate- ful," he said, " but I do hope you will not attribute my present position to anything you have done."

" Oh, but I can not believe it," she replied earnestly, casting upon him a look of great grati- tude. " But for your effort to serve me, I am sure you would not now be in this predicament. You did not get my notes last night. I feared this, and therefore wrote you."

" I did not receive them until too late to respond, and this morning, before I could go to you, I was compelled to call upon Captain Lawton."

" Captain Lawton,—I knew it. I knew it was my fault."

She told him with strict accuracy her interview with the Captain the day previous. Jack listened attentively, and when she had finished said :

" I presume that interview preceded my sum- mons. But I should not have escaped. You were under surveillance. The man who annoyed me when I called upon you to deliver the package, and who twice sauntered so close to us, was undoubt- edly a police spy. He saw the delivery of the package, and your call the day before on the Cap- tain gave the reason for supposing the package I gave you was the one you were seeking for, espe- cially after you wrote to say that you had recovered your letters."

" Yes, but you see all that directed attention to

you. So I am the cause of your trouble. Oh, how could I have been so foolish as to have gone to Captain Lawton, or to have written to him !"

" I don't think it was the best-advised thing to have done. But I can not blame you, for you were naturally anxious about your letters."

" Oh, the letters ! I care nothing about them. What are they compared with the danger you are in ? I mean to tell all about them so that you may be taken from here. All the trouble they can bring me into, the worst they can do, is to lose me my home and make me labor for my food, and what is that compared with your imprisonment ?"

Jack was much moved by her solicitude for him— by the generous spirit of self-sacrifice she was manifesting.

" For Heaven's sake do nothing rash," he cried. " Are you sure they will not lead to something worse than loss of home—to compulsion to labor ?"

" What can they ?" she answered. " The fault I committed was against my father—against Dr. Sherman. The worst he can do will be to drive me from him. But what of that, if you are to lose your liberty, your life perhaps !"

Jack wondered at her words. It began to dawn upon him that Lucy was possessed of a large, generous, self-sacrificing nature. How was he to reconcile this with the killing of Renfrew ? The girl puzzled him—she always had.

She puzzled some one else, too, who was striving all he could to listen.

" But the death of Renfrew," said Jack, giving verbal expression to his thoughts unconsciously.

" I know I was very wicked there," she replied. " I know I actually felt joy when I heard he was dead, for I felt that I should escape from his extortious. That was my wickedness. But the joy was short-lived. I began to feel a great pity for him, that he should have been taken off in his sins, and anger against the person—"

She stopped short and looked at Jack appealingly, even as if she were frightened. Jack was amazed. Was it possible that this girl could have been guilty of the deed? She went on:

"No, no, I don't mean that. I mean I was sorry for him. But do not let us talk of what I felt. What can be done for you? What can I do to help you? Won't the telling of my secret help you?"

She looked imploringly at him, her great soft eyes filled with compassion and her face suffused with the glow of her ardor—of her desire to help him even at the expense of herself.

The great tenderness of the woman, her complete want of selfishness, was almost too much for Jack. His heart swelled, and it was with difficulty he could repress the tears striving to reach his eyes. A spirit of emulation rose, and he thought that this charming girl should not outdo him in unselfishness.

"Please, Miss Sherman, do understand this—I am in no danger. You entirely exaggerate my situation. Doubtless it is true, that my summons to see Captain Lawton—that the knowledge I had a remote relation to the death of Renfrew by calling on him the day of the murder, may be traced to our conversation in the B—— Hotel, when I delivered the package to you; if you desire to go further, perhaps to the fact of your call upon the Captain. But, admitting all this, still it has nothing whatever to do with my confinement here."

Lucy was astonished, and her face bore an expression of incredulity, perhaps also of disappointment, for, as contradictory as it may appear, she had felt a joy in the anticipation of making a sacrifice for the one who had served her so well.

"It is true, Miss Sherman, I assure you,"

continued Jack; "let me tell you how it came
about."

Briefly reciting his visit to the detective, he told
the episode of the recognition of the pistol with
great particularity.

Lucy listened eagerly.   The color in her cheeks,
her glistening eyes and her parted lips telling vividly
her excitement.   She breathed rapidly, even turning
pale, as Gordon repeated the remark of the detective, " You are either the murderer, or the one
witness who can point directly to the person who
did the deed."

" Well," said Gordon, continuing, " I am not the
murderer, and I take it if any one is foolish enough
to make that charge against me I can easily dis-
prove it.   As to the pistol I recognized, by which
it is said Renfrew was killed, it points to—by
Heaven !   If that is so, how can—"

He had broken off in his speech, because of a
thought which had overcome and filled him with
gladness.   Why had he not thought of that before ?   If his fears or suspicions were correct, Lucy
could not have killed Renfrew—a wild joy possessed
him.   It seemed as if his whole being was flooded
with light.   He stopped and looked at Lucy beaming at him through her tears.   Of course she was
not guilty of the deed.   How could he have brought
himself to suppose she was ?

Lucy was waiting for him to complete her joy.
He had not killed Jacob—Cyril.   How could she
ever have supposed so good and kind a man could
have done so ?

" Oh, please, go on ! " she cried, her eyes swimming in moisture, and the love-light glimmering
through her tears.   " You did not kill him, and—"

Jack bent a strange look upon her.   What did
she mean ? . Could she have thought he had done
it ?   This was, indeed, a strange complication.   He

was even greatly pleased ; no, he was overjoyed at the tnought she had entertained a suspicion he was the murderer, for it was confirmation she had not done it. He was conscious there was a want of proper moral spirit in all this, but in the rush of joy and excitement, he could not stop to analyze the strange situation.

Lucy was waiting for him—hanging on his lips.

" I recognized the pistol," he continued, " as similar to one possessed by a woman of my acquaintance. If it had been any other pistol than the one it was, I should not have given a second thought to it. But it is a rare one, picked up abroad. Yet I can not bring my mind to believe that this woman could have had any connection with Renfrew,— much less with his murder. It is because I refused to say toward whom my suspicion traveled, that I am confined. You see you are not responsible for my being here."

" Oh, I am so glad," she exclaimed feebly. The truth was, she was not satisfied that he was making a sacrifice for some other woman. Then she added, as if unconscious she was speaking aloud, " Any one but you ! Any one but you !"

Jack cast upon her a strange look. She was in a profound study.

He said in a low tone in which there was not a particle of reproach :

" Lucy."

The girl started at the word and tone, and looked him full in the face.

" Lucy," he went on, with a world of tenderness in his voice. " I think you must have believed I committed the deed."

The blood rushed into her face, suffusing her temples, and there was a shy, soft, appealing look in her eyes. She rose and would have walked away from him.   He stood up, and taking her hands, gently detained her.

" Is it so ? " he asked.

" Oh ! " trying to hide her confusion, " I only feared so.   I feared there had been a quarrel—a quarrel over my letters.   And—if it were so, I owed you so much."

" I am afraid our moral senses have been blunted of late," said Jack, smiling. "Well, I can not confess to the murder, but I will make a confession to you now, that I have always intended to make when the proper time came.   There can not be, there never will be, a better time than now."

Without further ado he told her all, from the beginning—from the first time he saw her in a restaurant, when he made her the subject of a bet, until he had delivered the package to her.

Lucy listened with astonishment, annoyed, ashamed at times.

When he had finished his tale, he stood holding her hands; she trying to avoid a gaze she could not but feel was ardent and penetrating.

" Well ! " he said after a time.   " You say nothing ?   Am I not to be forgiven ? "

" Forgive you," she said, her rich voice trembling with tenderness and agitation.   " Forgive you ? Oh, Mr. Gordon, what have I to forgive ? I can give you thanks—thanks from the bottom of a very grateful heart—a heart so full of gratitude you can not know.   To think you were so good, so noble as to interfere for a friendless, tortured creature, whom you did not even know.   It was noble ; it was disinterested."

" Disinterested ! " said Jack with a sort of a caressing laugh.   " I am afraid not.   No, I'm afraid I was very much interested from the moment I saw you in the restaurant."

"Oh, no, no," cried Lucy, struggling to release her hands.

"But yes, yes," said Jack, retaining them. "It must out, Lucy. I have tried to deny it to my-self. But there never has been a time when your voice had not the power to thrill me to the center. I have struggled against it, I have tried to smother my passion, I know it now, but here it is blazing furiously, consuming me. Oh, Lucy, why should I deny I love you?"

"Oh, don't, please, please don't. You do not know."

"I know enough. I know I love you. I know it is a singular place to woo in. And I know when a young woman comes with love and tenderness in her eyes, her voice vibrating with sympathy and anxiety for a young man in trouble, that young man were worse than a coward, if he did not then try to seize the happiness within his reach."

"Oh, Mr. Gordon—"

"Which his name is Jack."

"You do not know. How can you think of giv-ing your love to one who has acknowledged to you she has committed a crime and carries it as a tor-turing secret?"

"Fault was what I believe you called it."

"Fault when committed—a crime now in its continuance."

"Whatever it was, dear Lucy, it has, I am sure, long since been repented. Whatever it is I now condone."

Lucy looked up at him, her face glorified, her eyes swimming in tears. She had committed a crime, she had repented,—now she was to make expiation.

"No, Mr. Gordon, I shall not give you the burden of that crime. The consequences of it I must bear alone. I will not mar your life as I have marred

my own.   I will not permit you to take a wife
whom you must despise if you know the truth,
whom you must always distrust if she share not that
secret with you.   Later on you will recognize this,
and then you will know that in part at least I have
repaid you for the great service you have done
me—for what you have suffered for me.   I shall
not be silly and fail to tell you that I do not appreciate the tender of your noble love.   Do not think
I do not know I am making a sacrifice.   How
much I desire your esteem you may learn when I
humiliate myself by telling you, and begging you
to believe, that this fault, this crime does not affect
my maiden purity."

Jack was much affected by her earnestness.

"I care not what it is," he cried.   " I love you
and I know that you love me.   Fate has drawn us
together, and we are not to be separated.   A power
stronger than ourselves has done this.   Why struggle against it ?   As I stand here pleading as for my
life, I know from the time I first saw you I loved you."

He took her in his arms before she was aware
what he was about to do.   She struggled for a
moment, but the powerful arms infolding her were
too strong, and she yielded, not so much after all to
his strength as to her passion.

It was but for a moment, however.   With an
effort she released herself.

"No, no," she cried, "it will not do.   I am
right.   You are wrong."

" Let me be the judge," urged Jack.   " That one
embrace, yielding as you did only for a moment,
tells me louder than words that my love is returned.
Tell me the secret, and let me be the judge of
my own fate."

She looked up at him shyly, and saw a strong,
glowing, deeply earnest face bending over her—a
face to be trusted with her life.

"It shall be so," she said. "When you are free come to me and I will tell you all. I will tell you, and you will then leave me to my misery, the world darker than before."

" I am content," replied Jack, and he bent over her and impressed a warm kiss upon her forehead.

She went away trembling with excitement and happiness. · Jack walked to his room as if treading on air.

Shortly after she drove away, the Captain issued from the jail.

" Well, well, well !" he said as he walked away. " That was an experience. These two people have had nothing to do with it. But who is the woman Gordon suspects ? It will be hard to make him tell, for he is not common stuff."

CHAPTER XVII.

ADMIRABLE OBSTINACY.

GORDON was not left long to dwell upon the scene through which he had just passed, nor to give much thought to the fault Lucy regarded as an insuperable bar to their union. As a matter of fact he gave the latter little weight, believing it to be some venial offense which she, in her innocence, had exaggerated into a great fault. The important thing was that he loved this beautiful creature and she had acknowledged her love in return.

The announcement of other visitors caused him to put aside his pleasing thoughts and prepare to welcome them. To his great surprise he found them to be his friends "Dizzy" Lowell and his sister, Miss Appleby, and Will Robb.

These young people made a great outcry as they entered, and Jack, who was inclined to believe curiosity had led them to the jail, was not over well pleased.

"What puzzles me," said Jack, repressing his displeasure, "is how you came to know I was here so quickly."

"Easily explained," replied Will Robb. "We were on our way to a matinée, and meeting your man Crimmins nearly distracted, we got it out of him and so came to you instead, to see if we could do anything."

"Ah, that explains it," said Jack, " I wish Crimmins had been as industrious in getting my clothes here as he has been in spreading the news of my being locked up."

" Why," exclaimed Miss Appleby, " are you going to stay here long ? "

" The period of my stay is somewhat indefinite. I don't know. I am here, however."

" But what is the meaning of it all ? " said Mollie Lowell, solicitude plainly apparent on her pretty face.

" Did you ever know, Mollie," said Jack, " how dangerous it was to be suspected of being too well informed ? "

" No."

" It is ; and you see before you an evidence of the truth of the remark."

" But I don't understand."

" Then I'll enlighten you. I made a call on the detective who has charge of ferreting out the murderer of Renfrew the actor, this morning, and while talking about it he showed me an article which is closely connected with the murder and by the means of which he expects to trace the doer of the deed. This article I recognized at once, and the detective, perceiving the recognition, demanded to know to whom it belonged. Not knowing all the circumstances I refused to tell. Consequently I am here as an important witness—*in re* Renfrew case—I believe that is the way the lawyers put it."

" Pshaw ! " said Miss Appleby in profound disgust. " Why didn't you tell and end it ? "

" What ? and involve a lady of high degree in a scandal ? That wouldn't have been nice, Lou."

" I would," said Mollie. " I wouldn't be locked up in jail for any trumpery woman."

" My dear Mollie," said Jack, laughing, " I haven't known you all your life without learning that that is just what you would do for a friend, Yes, go to jail and stay there too,"

"Pooh! No, I wouldn't," replied that young lady, glancing about the room. "Not that this looks to me as I supposed a jail did. I thought it was all stone walls and chains and bars. This appears like a third-rate hotel at a watering-place. You don't seem to be much frightened, Jack?"

"No, there is nothing to be frightened about. But I am angry all the way through."

"You can't stay here, Jack," said Miss Appleby. "What are you going to do about it?"

"Well, I am here," said Jack. "But," and a hard, stern look came upon his face as he continued, "this dance isn't over yet. My turn will come some time, and then I'll find out whether a man can be locked up at the pleasure of anybody who wears brass buttons."

"You ought to get a lawyer," said Will Robb.

"I don't want one," replied Jack shortly. "Let them go on. There'll be fight enough before all is over, Will. Let me alone for that."

"Are you sure about that article?" asked Mollie Lowell.

"Quite. There can be no mistake about it."

"I'd tell then, for it must be an awful bore to stay here."

"Which advice I decline with thanks. After the way they have tried to force me, I'd remain here for the rest of my life before I'd tell."

"I say, Jack," said Dizzy, who had been profoundly thinking while the others were chattering. "You are here because you won't speak?"

"Yes."

"And you are going to stay here rather than tell?"

"Precisely."

"And it's because you don't want a lady's name made public?"

"Yes."

" And that is because you doubt whether she did for Renfrew ? "

" You have the idea exactly."

" Well, I think you are going about it the right way to drag her name into public talk."

" How, my sapient youth ? "

" Why, it can't be long before those paper fellows will get on to your confinement here. Then they'll go poking around until they find out what the article is, describe it, and some fellow will drop to it and give it away, and then the whole thing'll be out. Better get out of this, and you will be able to do something outside."

" Dizzy " had presented a view of the matter Jack had not taken.

Mollie, who had been listening, got up and going to him kissed him, saying :

" Why, ' Dizzy,' you're very wise. Never again shall I call you dull."

" Tell you what," said " Dizzy," struggling to free himself from his sister's caress, "Will, you take the girls home and I'll go after Mr. Van Huyn. He's a friend of ours, and has got a big head."

To this Jack, by making no reply, gave acquiescence. And the rest, after many expressions of good will, went off.

" Dizzy " soon returned with Mr. Van Huyn, and that lawyer listened attentively to Jack's recital of the events of the day.

" There are some points you have not made clear," said Mr. Van Huyn, after Jack had finished, " and I must ask you some questions."

" Very well," said Jack, "but I warn you there are some you may ask which I will not answer."

The lawyer bent a suspicious glance upon Jack, as he remarked :

" A client should conceal nothing from his lawyer, if he expects to have intelligent assistance."

" Perhaps.   But go on with your questions, Mr. Van Huyn.   Let us see how we come out."

The lawyer evidently was not well pleased with the manner in which Jack answered him.   After a moment's thought he said :

" What acquaintance had you with Renfrew prior to your call upon him ? "

" None whatever."

" Your call upon him was then one of business ? "

" Entirely so.   The business of another person."

" And that business was in behalf of—"

" That is a question I can not answer," replied Jack firmly.

• " Nor one as to the nature of the business ? "

" No, except this far.   It was to demand the return of letters written by the one on whose behalf I went to see Renfrew, who was making bad use of them."

" Um.   What time in the day did you call upon Renfrew ? "

" About three o'clock.   But, pardon me, Mr. Van Huyu, this line of questioning is useless, if you will permit me to say so.   The police authorities do not connect me, or the person in whose behalf I went, with the murder.   That my calling upon that particular day was merely coincidental they are abundantly satisfied."

" Why then did they send for you ? " asked the lawyer sharply, considerably annoyed by the way in which Jack checked him.

" Because, having difficulty in learning anything about Renfrew's habits of life and friends—surroundings—they erroneously concluded, taking my call upon him as evidence of familiarity with him, I might tell them.   That I could tell them nothing Captain Lawton soon became convinced.   The event which led to my confinement here occurred subsequently."

" The recognition of the pistol ? "

" Yes. That is the beginning. All that goes before only leads up to my being in the Captain's office where I could see and recognize the pistol, and has no bearing upon my being here except in that way."

" I see. You refused to tell who it belonged to."

" Yes. I refused to say anything."

" The detective was right in demanding information. Why did not you tell him ? "

" Because I would not blindly involve a person for whom I had a high respect in an unpleasant publicity. Let me submit a case," said Jack, rising and pacing up and down the room. " Suppose you knew a lady whose standing in society was high, whose life was so correct as to be a model for all wives, who enjoyed the esteem of every one who was acquainted with her, whose daily walk and life was as irreproachable as that of the lady who honors you by bearing your name,"—the lawyer bowed in response to these words, as if thanking Jack. " Suppose, I say, you knew such a lady, and knew that several years previous she had possessed a pistol that had been used subsequently to kill a man. Would you immediately cry out that she had committed the murder?"

" No. But would such a charge follow in this case ? "

" I do not know that it would. But I think it quite likely. But what unquestionably would occur would be that her name would be brought into connection with a scandalous case, for such I assure you it will turn out to be, Mr. Van Huyn, when all sorts of vulgar people would indulge in coarse speculations as to her probable connection with this fellow Renfrew."

" I presume that is so."

" What do I know about it that I should give

tongue to it?" continued Jack warmly. "I only know that seven years ago—say six—she owned this pistol and another just like it. She may have lost them, sold them, given them away. They may have been stolen from her. Now without having an opportunity to learn anything about her posses- sion of them, I am expected, simply because a beast of a detective demands to know, to blurt out the name of a high-bred, refined woman, whose life is of the highest, and surround her name with a cloud of suspicion—a woman who has shown me no end of kindness, who has welcomed me to her home and at her board, who has been my consistent friend from boyhood. It may be law and justice, as lawyers and courts see it, but I'll be d—d if I will. I don't care what the consequences may be. I may be a party to the crime then, but I'll be a man of honor and a gentleman. I won't talk, and all the detectives, and all the judges, and all the courts, and all the jails can't make me."

"Good!" shouted "Dizzy," springing across the room at a bound and grasping Jack's hand. "You're a trump—you're a daisy. I'll back you sixty to one." With his pink cheeks pinker than ever, he retired to his chair, and thrusting the handle of his cane in his mouth, he turned to listen to what the lawyer would say in response.

"Then I understand that, until you have a better basis of suspicion than is involved in the mere recognition of the pistol, you refuse to speak?"

"Certainly, until I know more than I do at pres- ent."

"Such sacrifice of self is not usual, Mr. Gordon," said the lawyer, in whose altered tones there was evidence of the admiration he felt for the young man's spirit. "I think the detective has traveled a little beyond his power, considered from a strictly legal point. It is, however, customary to arrest an important witness and hold him, especially if he is thought to be an unwilling one, or inclined to the other side. The ease with which an arrest can be accomplished under due process of law, and that in ninety-nine cases out of a hundred public opinion will justify the act, has caused the authorities to ignore the steps necessary to a strictly legal confinement. However, it seems to me the course to follow, at first, is for me to see the detective and protest against your confinement. This may be sufficient to secure your release. After that we will determine whether it is necessary to get out a writ of *habeas corpus.* I'll go at once."

He went off, leaving "Dizzy" behind with Jack.

"Say, old man," cried "Dizzy," as soon as the door was closed behind the lawyer. "You're a high-stepping, rangy colt, now I tell you. Never you mind, we'll pull you through. I'll make a book against all odds on that. Say, you know that colt—Leamington stock—I bought from Cap. Connor, made 1.48½ this morning in practice, Jimmie up, Little Billet leading, and the General urging. I'll give him to you when you get out of this."

"Dizzy" had gone to the extreme in testifying his admiration for Jack's conduct, all of which Jack appreciated, and so, there being nothing further to say upon the subject, they fell to talking of horses. Thus they were engaged when Mr. Van Huyn returned,—not alone, however, for he was accompanied by both Captain Lawton and the Inspector.

"Mr. Gordon," said the lawyer, "I have talked with these gentlemen, and have convinced them that no necessity exists for locking you up; that you have no intention of leaving the city, and will give your word to that effect."

" I'll give it to you, Mr. Van Huyu," said Jack stiffly.

The Captain attempted to speak, but the Inspector checked him, saying :

" That will be entirely sufficient on that head, Mr. Van Huyn."

" It is, however, required of you," continued the lawyer, "that you will satisfy yourself as to the possession of the pistol, and if it has within three months passed out of the hands of the lady who owned it when you last knew anything of it, you will immediately inform the Captain, and tell him, if you can, into whose possession it went. If not, then the name of the lady who owned it, whose name you now refuse to give."

" I'll make no such pledge to you, nor to any one else," answered Jack firmly.

" Right you are, my daisy!" cried " Dizzy," very pink.

The Inspector turned upon that young man with a scowl, but its effect was not startling, since " Dizzy" winked at him, as if he thought the Inspector approved Jack's obstinacy.

" No, Mr. Van Huyu," said Jack, ignoring the presence of the two officials. " If I go from here I go free and unbound by promise or pledge. I will not leave the city, but that is all I will pledge."

" Dizzy" performed a tattoo with the end of his cane upon the floor by way of applause.

Mr. Van Huyn and the two detectives retired into a corner for consultation, which was for a time very earnest. It had continued for some minutes, when Mr. Van Huyn turned to Jack with an air of satisfaction.

" These gentlemen," he said, "do not press the requirement. . Therefore, you are free to go ; but I desire you to fully understand that I have given my personal word that you will not leave the city, and you will not cause these gentlemen any trouble because of your confinement here."

Jack bit his lips and hesitated. " Dizzy " took his cane from his mouth and looked anxiously at Jack.

" Since you have given your word, Mr. Van Huyu," replied Jack, " I'll stand by it. But such was not my intention."

" Dizzy " applauded again with the end of his cane.

" Then," said the Inspector, " you are free to go."

The detectives departed ; in a short time the others followed, Jack having been delayed by the ceremonies of release.

" Dizzy " was overjoyed at the result, and again and again cried out :

" See, we did pull you through."

He was so elated over Jack's admirable resoluteness in refusing to give expression to his suspicions, that he insisted on giving a dinner at the Hoffman House to all who had assisted in " pulling Jack through."

While Mr. Van Huyn, who was the principal "puller," could not be persuaded to participate in the feast, which " Dizzy " promised should be " bang up," with the best of wines, Jack could not well escape, though he would have been better pleased to have spent a part of the evening with Lucy.

All that was permitted him was a brief note to her, informing her of his release and his intention to call upon her the following day. He closed his eventful day merrily at the table, around which were gathered his four staunch friends, Miss Appleby, Will Robb, Mollie Lowell and her brother.

CHAPTER XVIII.

REMINISCENCES WITH A PURPOSE.

IT was an hour at which most men lunched that Jack breakfasted on the morning following the evening on which " Dizzy " gave what he was pleased to term his " feed " in honor of his friend's release.

Although it was early for a call, still, relying upon his intimate footing in the house, he determined as soon as he finished his meal to visit Mrs. Jamieson. Half an hour later found him in her parlors. The lady soon came to him, and in a ravishing demi-toilette and with an air of anxious solicitude.

" Gracious, Jack ! " she said on seeing him, " I hope nothing serious has occurred again. Come into the library, where we will not be interrupted by callers, if there should be any."

Leading the way, she took him into the apartment named and said :

" Make yourself as comfortable as you can. How do you feel ? Are you all broken up with your experience ? Were you much frightened ? "

" What are you referring to ? " asked Jack in return, not a little astonished by her words.

" Why, about that horrible mistake of arresting you as the murderer of Renfrew."

Jack laughed aloud.

" It is pleasant to hear that. Where did you learn that interesting news ? "

" Why, Mrs. Van Huyn was here this morning

telling me about it, and very loud in her praises of your manliness. Her husband told her about it."

"I should like to have her version," said Jack, partly amused and partly vexed.

"Isn't it true? She said that those horrid detectives got it into their stupid heads that you committed the murder and arrested you; that after they talked with you they found out you didn't, but that you knew who did but wouldn't tell, and then they put you in jail."

"I am afraid Mrs. Van Huyn has not properly quoted her husband, and I don't think there would have been anything particularly manly in my refusing to tell the name of the murderer if I had known it. No, I was not suspected of the murder; and I was confined because, having knowledge of a matter connected with it, I refused to speak, since it would have involved the name of a friend in a scandal. That's all."

"That is very different," said the little lady. "How does it feel to be in jail?"—with a shudder.

Jack laughed a low, happy laugh.

"I never was so happy anywhere. I give you my word, Mrs. Jamieson, I would not have missed going to that jail, had I known what was to happen, for all things the future might promise me."

Mrs. Jamieson looked at him curiously and waited for him to go on, while a happy smile played about Jack's lips. An intuition warned the lady that she ought not to push inquiries.

"You always were a queer creature, Jack," she said. "The idea of being happy in jail. I am glad it was no worse. I was much frightened for you."

The conversation now drifted into other channels, until Jack, seizing a favorable opportunity, turned it in the direction of the object of his call.

"Do you recollect the winter," he inquired,

" I spent with you and Mr. Jamieson in the south of Europe ? "

" Shall I ever forget it, Jack ? I go back to it again and again. What perfectly happy days they were ! Ah, me ! how the time flies. It is seven years ago. What a nice boy you were in those days ! Just a fresh, enthusiastic boy, without any affectations."

" Oh, I was fresh enough, I'll warrant," laughed Jack. "A mere lad—only twenty."

" With your pockets full of money your poor old father had lavished on you. Money you wanted to spend on every conceivable thing you saw. Dear, dear ! The worry you were to Walter and myself ! I had to take your money from you every time you went out alone."

" Yes, I recollect you kept me on short commons."

" Then your faculty for falling in love. How many times did I have to rush in and rescue you ? I was talking to Walter only a day or two ago about it."

" You have not forgotten that trip to the mountains when there were rumors of brigands, nor how frightened you were about them ? "

" Don't recall my silliness. Walter teases me about it to this day."

" Nor the armament I purchased with which to defend ourselves."

The little lady burst into a peal of merriment.

" Shall I ever forget the comical sight you presented that evening in Florence, when you came in loaded down—"

" With loaded things, eh ?" interrupted Jack. " Do you remember that brace of pistols with curiously carved ivory handles I bought for you ? "

" No, nor how you wanted to take me into the palace garden to teach me how to shoot them off."

"Have you got them yet?" inquired Jack, carelessly.

At this moment Mr. Jamieson entered the room and greeted Jack warmly.

"There is the culprit," exclaimed Mrs. Jamieson. "Call him to account."

"What is it?" asked her husband.

"Jack was asking if I still had those quaint pistols with curiously carved ivory handles he bought for me in Florence. I refer him to you for explanation."

"Jack," said that gentleman, with mock seriousness, "you have touched upon a sore spot. My life for two years has been made miserable, my home a ——" pointing downward—"you know, all on account of those useless toys you gave to the partner of my woes. If I had taken the two children who call her mother and lost them somewhere in the wilds of New Jersey, I would not have heard so much about it as I have about the loss of those miserable pistols."

"That is not giving Jack the information he asks," said the lady, with a contemptuous toss of her head. "Now listen, Jack. About two years ago I loaned them, with some other rare and curious things, to a lady who was giving a loan exhibition in aid of some charity."

"You see," interrupted Mr. Jamieson, "the old story. The original sin was committed by the woman. Now if she—"

"Be quiet, and don't interrupt," demanded the imperative little dame, stamping a diminutive foot upon the floor. "She took them, promising the best of care of them. So proud of them was I, so highly did I value them, not alone for their association, but also for their beauty and rarity, that on the night the exhibition closed, I sent Walter after them and the other things."

" Yes, it cost me a dollar to get in ten minutes before the door closed," said Mr. Jamieson mournfully. " I have lamented that dollar ever since."

" When he came back I told him to lay the things down in this room on the table in the corner. Several days after, when I came to look them over to restore them to their proper places, the pistols were not to be found. Asking him where they were, and other things also missing, what, suppose you, was his answer ? "

" I don't know, I am sure," replied Jack, manifesting an interest in the recital hardly justified.

" He did not know. He had loaned them, the night he brought the other things home, to some one, but who, he couldn't recollect. Somebody who was going to have tableaux, or private theatricals."

" Now, Jack," said her husband, " you have the story of an event which has caused many heartaches in this house. If you should hear, one morning, that in a rash moment I had ended my life, you will know the reason."

" Mr. Jamieson," said Jack, so gravely as to excite the attention of the others, " will you answer a question seriously ? Much depends upon it, I assure you."

They looked at him in surprise.

" Do you indeed not recollect to whom you gave those pistols ? "

" I do not indeed. Mrs. Jamieson does not tell you all. I loaned a number of articles that evening. To whom the pistols were given I could never recollect. The other articles were all returned in good time. The pistols never. It was several weeks after before my wife spoke of missing them, and though I remembered loaning them, I could not tell to whom. Why do you ask ? "

" I think you ought to know," said Jack, after

a moment's reflection. " Renfrew, the actor, was killed with one of those pistols."

Both were greatly shocked.

" How do you know that ? " asked Mr. Jamieson, after he had recovered from his astonishment.

" I recognized it when I saw it in the hands of the detective."

" Was this the reason—was it because you refused to tell who you thought it belonged to, that you were locked up ? " asked Mrs. Jamieson.

" Oh, that is an old story now," said Jack uneasily.

The lady rose from her chair, and, taking Jack's hand, said :

" It was very noble of you, Jack. I appreciate it. You have done me a service I shall never forget. You have saved me from a great deal of ugly talk."

The tears stood in her eyes. Mr. Jamieson did not understand, and so Mrs. Jamieson told him the story of Jack's refusal to tell. When it was finished he said to Jack :

" Gordon, that was the act of a true and unselfish friend. As the little woman says, you have saved her from a great deal of ugly talk, and though I could have explained all, still explanations do not follow close on suspicions. I thank you most gratefully. Few men would have been unselfish or courageous enough to have faced the possible consequences."

" Pooh ! pooh ! " cried Jack, feeling very red and uncomfortable. " The obligations are all on the other side. It was very little to do in return for all the kindness and friendship I have had at the hands of Mrs. Jamieson and yourself."

Seizing the first opportunity, he hurried away to escape their protestations of gratitude. He felicitated himself again and again that he had not been betrayed into revealing Mrs. Jamieson's name under the circumstances, and he thought that a deeper mystery had settled on the case. Dismissing further thought of the matter, he hastened to Lucy, filled with pleasurable anticipations.

CHAPTER XIX

LUCY'S CRIME.

THE letter announcing Jack's release was received by Lucy with surprise and delight. She had been in a flutter of excitement ever since she left Jack in the morning. His declaration of love had filled her with happiness, though she by no means felt it was to continue. Hanging over her was the dread of the result of her avowal to him of that fault—that crime she had committed. Through her love and gratitude, and because of her admiration for him, she so magnified, in her own eyes, the noble qualities and keen sense of honor of her lover, she made sure her revelation would shock and disgust him, and that he would fly from her. Notwithstanding the happiness she felt over his love for her, she was miserable whenever she thought of the necessity of that tale. Sometimes she wished she had not told him at all, but had let events take their course. Let him love and be loved in return, with her mysterious connection with Renfrew unexplained. Yet when her commonsense came uppermost she knew that such a course was impossible. When she thought of the misery she had endured the past three years she was glad she had not permitted herself to drift into another deception. To leave the misery unexplained and to marry him would be to give cause for suspicion and distrust from the beginning. No, she would not deceive him. She preferred to lose him to doing that. He deserved all the good she could give him, and she would not repay his kindness and his love with deceit. This was the burden of her thought when she fell asleep and when she awoke in the morning.

Lucy regarded Dr. Sherman's absence from town as fortunate, since she could entertain Jack in their own parlors, free from the intrusion of strangers. To secure herself from any interruption whatever, she instructed her maid to go to the office immediately after Gordon's arrival, and announce that Miss Sherman was out for the day.

Accordingly when Jack presented his card at the desk of the B—— hotel he found the way open for him. In after years he thought Lucy never looked more beautiful than she did that afternoon, when she rose to greet him, evidently attired for the event. It was not, however, her attire which in his opinion heightened her beauty. It was the modesty of her demeanor, the happy light in her eyes, and the warm, bashful blushes covering her cheeks.

"You can not tell," she said, "what pleasure your note gave me last night. I should not have rested comfortably if I had supposed you were still confined in that horrid jail!"

"Don't call it horrid," replied Jack. "It was in that blessed jail I found my senses and my happiness."

Lucy blushed again and toyed with a rose she had taken from the table.

"You did not tell me how you were released so soon. I am anxious to know."

So Jack was again compelled to tell the story.

"Are you satisfied as to the truth of your suspicions?" she asked.

"Upon the contrary, I am satisfied all suspicion in that direction was misplaced. I have felicitated myself over and over again that I did not mention the lady's name. Her husband satisfied me the pistols passed by his own act out of her keeping two years ago."

Lucy felt greatly relieved to find that the lady for whom Jack had made his sacrifice owned a husband of her own, for she had entertained a feeling of no little jealousy toward the unknown. She became more gay, and the conversation now drifted into a channel the import of which, entertaining to the participants, has no bearing on our story.

The afternoon passed rapidly,—a fact of which Jack was made conscious by the sudden flaring of the electric lights in the street. So he approached abruptly the object he had at heart.

" Lucy," he said, moving his chair closer to her and taking her hand. " I want your consent to speak to your father. Why should we delay our happiness ? "

The girl withdrew her hand from his quickly, and looking down remained silent. The crucial time for her had come.

" You know I love you, you have confessed your love for me. Why put obstacles in our way?" asked Jack.

" Oh, Mr. Gordon," replied Lucy, her voice trembling and the color flying from her face, " there is an obstacle—a serious obstacle. So great a one that all the hope there is left me is, that I can still count you as a friend."

" Lucy, my love, that is impossible," pleaded Jack. " I must be something more than a friend to you. A friend always, but something nearer and dearer. We love each other, and surely you must see that it must be all or nothing."

" Yes, I know," she replied, the tears coming into her eyes. " It was a thoughtless speech. It were better to part now, while I still have your respect and esteem."

"That is quite as impossible," said Jack, firmly. "I won you fairly as ever man won his love. Why should I give you up? Indeed, I would be unworthy the love of any woman, and certainly of yours, if I were to leave, content with this dismissal, while you do not deny your own love."

He had possessed himself of her hand again and was pressing it to his lips, an act of which she seemed to be unconscious, so profound in thought was she. Suddenly, however, she drew it from him, and springing to her feet said:

"Oh, Mr. Gordon, how can you treat me so? You are cruel. You have won the secret of my love from me—a secret I meant to have kept to myself. Why do you tempt me? Can you not see that it is through my love that I am endeavoring to act honorably toward you? That I would save you from the burden of a wife who is unfit for you—for whom you can have nothing but horror when you know her past. Did I love you less I could accept your love and deceive you. But I can't. I love you too well, and I am trying—oh, so hard!—to do my duty to you. If you have no pity for me, have pity for yourself, and fly from me."

She walked to the window, completely unnerved, and looked out upon the street.

Jack followed her and stood respectfully beside her, while he waited for her to become more calm. When she seemed more composed, he took her hand and leading her to the sofa, seated her and placed himself beside her.

"Lucy," he said quietly, "I think your conscience is very tender, and that you have become morbid over a fault many people would have long ago forgotten."

"No, no, no!" she said. "You do not know how bad it is."

"The girl who tells the man she loves she can not become his wife, because of some fault she has committed, can not have a vicious heart."

"Oh, you do not know! You do not know!"

"You recollect," he said tenderly, "I was to be the judge."

"Oh, yes," replied Lucy, nervously, "but I've thought it all over. I can not tell you—I do not dare. And I do so want your respect."

"I owe you a great deal," said Jack, "for giving me the priceless pearl of your love, but, Lucy, I owe myself something. I have a duty to myself to perform. Do you suppose I can let all the glorious vision of the happiness which burst upon me when I knew you loved me fade away and make no effort to turn it into reality? Do you suppose I could retain my own self-respect and make no effort to secure for myself that warm, loving heart of yours? Do you suppose I can be content, or that I ought to be content, to go away now without better reason?"

"But you don't know how—"

"No, I don't know, that is true. But I can look into your eyes and read that it is nothing. I can look into your pure face and see that wickedness does not reside there. Come. If it pains you, don't tell it. I'll put my trust in you, and we will never speak of it more."

"Oh!" cried Lucy, starting up again, "was ever a poor girl so tortured? And I am trying so hard to be good! If I do not tell him I will lose faith in myself; if I do, I will lose him."

"No," cried Jack, restraining her, and gently forcing her to sit down. "I do not love lightly. I have found that out. But," he added, almost sternly, "you shall choose now. Either you shall

or you shall not tell me. But in either event I go
to Dr. Sherman and ask for this hand. I will not
be denied."

"Oh, no, no, no!" cried Lucy, terror-stricken.
"Why can't you let me go? Why drive me to a
humiliating confession? Why force me to lose
both your esteem and your love? Go. Have some
mercy upon a poor girl who would lay down her
life to save you from harm. Accept the devotion
of my heart and go. Oh, why don't you go?"

"Why don't I go?" said Jack, his voice vibrating
with passion and emotion. "Why don't I go?
For the profoundest of reasons: I love you. Go?
Never. While strength is left me to sue for my
happiness, here I'll stay."

The masterfulness of her lover, his determination,
and the love glowing in his face gave her a sense
of keen pleasure, notwithstanding her wretched-
ness. She laid her hands upon his, looking long
into his radiant face, and said sadly:

"Oh, my love, my love, you master me! Here
then is my expiation. For love of you I sacrifice myself and go down into the dark waters of despair."

She slowly drew her hands from him, and lifting
them to her face covered her eyes. Jack looked
at her compassionately. He thought he read her
accurately when he determined that she would
never yield to her love until she had unburdened
herself. So profound was his trust in her that he
believed she exaggerated her offense; that when
it was told it would prove to be something he
could laugh away. He was sure she had become
morbid from dwelling long upon it. So he waited
patiently for her to begin. The early darkness
was beginning to close in upon them. The only
light was that given from the outside, and the fire
burning brightly in the grate.

Lucy withdrew her hands from her eyes, and

clasping them on her knee looked over them to the floor, but still did not speak. Jack was about to break the silence when she began.

"Dr. Sherman," she said, in a low, constrained voice, trembling with agitation, "is not my father. He adopted me when I was seventeen—five years ago. My name is Lucy Annesley. My father was a gentleman, my mother a lady, but they were poor—very poor—when I was born. My mother died long before I could recollect her. My father died when I was eight. I fell to the care of an uncle who lived in the Far West, who regarded me as a burden and placed me in a school,—Miss Waltham's, at Rocky Point,—and then left for his home without looking upon me."

"The inhuman wretch!" cried Jack.

"He paid my expenses, and paid them regularly until I was seventeen, when he said I was old enough to care for myself, and refused to maintain me longer. He wrote this to Miss Waltham. He never wrote to me, saw me, or sent me a message."

"He was heartless!" cried Jack.

"No, he considered me an unjust burden, that was all. When I had been at school four years, there came into it another scholar, like me alone and friendless in the world; an orphan, and, like me, supported through the charity of a relative, quite as unwillingly. Singularly her name was Lucy—Lucy Annesley. We became warm friends. But after two years she was happily released. She died, leaving all her poor earthly treasures and possessions to me. Ah, Lucy, Lucy, dear, why was it you? Why was it not I?"

Jack moved closely to her and laid his hand upon hers, but she gently removed it. It was an action which seemed to tell him to wait until he had heard her story.

"Two years later, when I was nearly sixteen, a

letter came to Miss Waltham from a gentleman abroad, asking about Lucy Annesley. It was from Dr. Sherman. Miss Waltham wrote him, giving him an account of me. This led to a correspondence with me which was continued for nearly a year, in which he hinted that the object of his inquiry and correspondence was to provide for my future. From the time my uncle cast me off, my future gave me anxiety, and I built largely on this prospect Dr. Sherman held out to me. I had but one relative except my uncle, and he was a cousin, a young man of twenty-four or five. He came to see me from time to time,—not often. And this cousin took great interest in the proposed action of Dr. Sherman. His name was Myers—Jacob Myers."

Jack started violently.

"Yes," continued Lucy sadly, "it was the one you knew as Cyril Renfrew. He had gone on the stage and adopted that name. As I grew near my seventeenth birthday there came a letter from Dr. Sherman, saying that he had arrived in New York and would within a week or two visit the school. It occurred that day that I looked into the box Lucy had left me, and for the first time I read the old love-letters of her mother, Lucy had treasured during her life. To my consternation I found it was the dead Lucy Dr. Sherman wanted ; that he had been a lover of her mother ; had written the letters ; and that Lucy's grandfather had refused to permit his daughter, Lucy's mother, to marry Dr. Sherman, but had forced her to wed a man named Annesley, who I have since learned was a distant cousin of my father. I was greatly disappointed."

" I should imagine so,"said Jack sympathetically.

"That afternoon my cousin visited me, and I told him of my crushed hopes. He made me bring him the box, and he read the letters. He asked many question about Lucy and whether any of her relatives were living. When he learned all were dead, he put the wicked idea into my head of not informing Dr. Sherman or Miss Waltham of my discovery."

"Ah!" said Jack; the fault was made clear to him.

"He urged me strongly. He painted my future in strong colors; pointed out the struggles and privations of poverty in the most unattractive way. Said that it would be flying in the face of Providence to fail to take advantage of the good fortune held out to me. He laughed at my opposition and qualms of conscience. He said there was a conspiracy of events in my favor; that it was no wrong; that Dr. Sherman wanted to do a benevolent act and I must not thwart him. He made me promise I would not inform Miss Waltham, and that I would not tell Dr. Sherman, until he saw me again. Then he wrote daily urging me not to undeceive the doctor, and visited me every two or three days, always urging me forward and arguing against my conscience. And, oh," said Lucy, turning a troubled and ashamed face on Jack, her eyes swimming in tears, "what could I, a poor, weak, inexperienced girl, who had never been twenty-four hours away from the seminary door, do against such advice and against a man of the world? Oh, Mr. Gordon, is it a wonder if I, frightened at the prospect of life as painted to me, presented and urged by this insidious counsel, proved to be weak?"

"No, no!" cried Jack, moved by her appeal to him. "A thousand times no!"

"But I did not yield at once. I debated and debated with myself, hesitating, delaying a conclusion, fearing to go forward, and, as the days grew, fearing

to go back, because I had not done it in the beginning when I first knew,—when, without warning, I
was called into the presence of Dr. Sherman. I
was so embarrassed and frightened I did not say
anything, for I could not, and Miss Waltham and
the doctor went on assuming that I was really the
one he sought. When I tried to speak it was too
late, and I was committed to the deception before I
had made up my mind what I should do. Then I
grew afraid, and so I have lived on. All the letters
to Jacob, which he used so wickedly, told the
whole story of my wicked deception. You know
the rest. And thus I have lived the lie, deceiving
Dr. Sherman, the adventuress Jacob called me—a
wicked, designing woman, too cowardly to tell the
truth, but bad enough to go on."

Lucy had borne up bravely as she told the story,
but now that it was finished, she threw her arms
on the back of the sofa and buried her head in
them

Jack permitted her to exhaust her emotion before
he spoke.

CHAPTER XX.

JACK AS A COUNSELOR.

LUCY had misinterpreted Jack's silence; she had persuaded herself the inevitable result of the story would be to drive him away from her, yet when she found he was silent, and, as she believed, because of her wickedness, the conviction came to her with all the sharpness of a new grief. She could not look upon him; she could not bear to encounter the disgust and horror she felt was pictured on his face. She wished he would go without a word and leave her to herself. All was over between them, and the sooner the end came the better.

When she had thrown her head upon her arms, she had turned her back to Jack, and he could not see her face. Presently he arose and, going to the other end of the sofa, he gently took her hands in his own, and said:

"Lucy! Lucy, my dear! Lucy, my love!"

She looked at him in wild amazement. In her misery was she losing her senses? Had he indeed called her " Love "? She looked into his eyes and saw there divine pity and love, so blended that it seemed to her in her despair the soul of an angel was looking through them. He said not a word, but he held out his arms to her. Overcome by surprise and emotion, she flung herself upon his breast and sobbed as if her heart would break.

"Come, Lucy, my love," said Jack at last. "Look up. There is no obstacle, after all."

"Oh, don't be kind to me," she said between her sobs, " if you don't mean to be ! "

" Mean to be ? " repeated Jack, with a low, happy laugh. " I mean to love you with my heart of hearts. Let me talk to you. It is true your fault is not what I supposed it to be. It is true, it is even graver than I supposed it to be. But, my love, I shall not blame you for its commission. Young, inexperienced, and placed in an almost unheard-of position, and urged thereto by one who should have advised you differently, I do not know that your act is to be wondered at. I shall not blame you, but if I were so disposed, it would be for not telling Dr. Sherman in after-years when you knew better."

She nestled in closer to him, her head still upon his breast.

" I often thought of doing it, but Dr. Sherman is so stern about such things, and Jacob said he would put me into prison, and that frightened me."

" Ah, I suppose," said Jack, " he did not want you to cease being a source of income to him. But, Lucy, I am surprised Dr. Sherman did not discover the imposition himself."

" I suppose," said Lucy, " I have told my story badly. Dr. Sherman is very sensitive about his love episode. He has grieved a great deal over it, and it has affected his whole life. He never talks about it. When I showed him the little box, with his letters to Lucy's mother and some little trinkets he had given her, he accepted it as proof of my birth, and said he was glad I had them, as he would not have to make further inquiries as to my identity, and thus would escape prying into his secrets. Nobody, therefore, knew that he adopted me for any other reason than that he fancied me, or that some relation existed between us. No one knew of his love for Lucy's mother, for it had been a secret, and he had lived abroad for twenty years."

"It is plain now," said Jack. " Truly it was, as your cousin said, a conspiracy of events to favor your step."

By this time Lucy had been restored to a condition approaching her usual composure, and began to realize it was far from the proper thing to be sitting with Jack's arms around her in a room lit only by a grate fire. So she disengaged herself from his embrace and lighted the gas. Having done so, she stole a shy, half-apologetic, half-appealing and wholly wondering glance at Jack. He interpreted it with the intuitive quickness of a woman.

Rising hastily he took her in his arms, and, before she divined his purpose, kissed her upon the lips, saying :

"Lucy, this is the seal of our engagement."

The warm blood rushed over her face, covering her neck.

"You still love me," she said with a soft glance, "after my confession ? "

" With all the warmth of this poor heart," he replied. " I never meant to let you go, Lucy. If your fault had been greater, it would have been the same, but it is far from irreparable. Dr. Sherman must be told of it."

Lucy shuddered.

" It will be a great shock to him," she said, " for he has grown fond of me in his way."

" Do you fear his anger ? "

" Yes ; he will not forgive me. He is relentless in his vengeance, and he will discard me. He will regard it all the more as a personal wrong since I have become necessary to his comfort."

" Then we must go about it diplomatically."

" I do not know what you mean."

"We shall not tell him until after we have obtained his sanction of our engagement—until after it has been announced and he is committed to it. Then he will have the interest of a third person to consider."

"Ah, but Jack, dear"—this was the first time she had called him so, and she was immediately rewarded—"all this will involve you in much annoyance, perhaps shame and humiliation. You will grow ashamed of your promised bride, I am afraid."

"My dear Lucy," replied Jack, laughing, "it is too late in the day for you to talk about involving me. You did that by existing. Why, you did it by going into that restaurant the first night I saw you."

She looked into his eyes anxiously, but saw nothing but love beaming in them.

"No, Lucy darling. I am certain now I loved you from the moment I first saw you. I regard you wholly as a victim of circumstances, alone in the world without proper guardians or counselors, and we'll fight our way together, hand in hand, please God. What causes me the most wonder is, how you came through all the stress and strain so unspoiled, so innocent, and so true-hearted. Your struggles are mine now, and while I do not pretend to any piety, I say, and say it fervently, I thank God for it."

Lucy, with eyes shining with love and admiration, said in reply :

"Oh, Jack, you are noble—you are a god."

"No, no," said Jack, laughing, "not a Greek god, certainly, with this nose—very common chap, I assure you, when you come to know me as I am."

"You are the god of my idolatry, Jack," she said shyly, her cheeks aflame. "You are my good angel. You have saved me from a great deal. You don't know how wicked I have been. Could you believe that I meant to kill myself on the Thursday night Jacob said I must bring the money?"

Jack looked at her incredulously, but Lucy so earnestly affirmed it he was forced to believe her. She told him of her scene with her cousin, and her determination and preparation to dispose of herself before exposure—a result frustrated by Renfrew's death.

"You were worked up into a highly nervous condition which did not permit you to see clearly," said Jack, quite horrified by the recital.

"I presume so. Poor Jacob, he paid the penalty of his evil-doing with his life."

"What do you know of his evil-doing?" asked Jack.

"Very little ; but Captain Lawton told me a number of letters had been found in his room showing he was extorting money from women in the basest way, for he had won their affections and compromised them. He asked me whether I knew a ' Dollie Dux?' I said no, of course, for it was such an absurd name. But, Jack, when you brought me my letters I found among them one signed by that name."

"Oh!" said Jack, "I hope you have burned your letters."

"Oh, yes, I burned all of mine. I saved the one written by ' Dollie Dux,' and why I hardly know. Let me show it to you ; it is a sad, pathetic letter."

She ran off into an adjoining department, and, quickly returning with it, handed it to Jack.

He looked over it hastily.

"Why," he exclaimed, "it is of date of the day before the murder!"

He read it aloud :

"DEAR CYRIL : I write you in an agony of tears.   Why do you torture me so ?   I have given you the best love of my heart, the love I have not given to any other man, not even my husband.   I have given you the pledge of it, for I have given you my honor.   More no woman can give, for when she has given that she has given all.   Yet you return this affection by cruelty and threats.   I can not give you any more money.   You must, you shall believe this.   If you must expose me, recollect that I have done all I could.   Heaven knows how truly I am speaking.   I have no means left.   All my jewels are in pawn and I am wearing imitations in their places, and tremble lest the deceit be discovered.   I am distracted.   Really I am bordering on insanity.   I am sure if you could see the nights I pass, how I walk the floor in an agony of fear and grief, longing for morning to come, to make another effort to secure money for you, only to find it impossible, you would have some pity for me.   I am growing desperate.   I can not face the disgrace of the terrible fall you threaten me with.   Oh, God, help my poor mother !   Do have some pity on me.

"I sign myself, not gayly, but as I am accustomed to,

"DOLLIE DUX."

"The infernal scamp !" said Jack, quivering with indignation.

"Oh, the poor, poor creature !" said Lucy.

"You say," asked Jack, "that Captain Lawton told you a number of such letters were found in his room ?"

"Yes, but that mine were not among them."

"No," replied Jack, "but they would have been had I not compelled him to give them up.   Evidently the police think that this is the woman who killed him."

"Oh, do you think so ?" asked Lucy, going over to Jack and looking over his shoulder.

"Yes, you see it is his latest intrigue."

"Why, Jack, that writing seems familiar to me.   Let me think."

"Don't think, Lucy," said Jack hastily, and folding the letter up.   "Put this letter away ; don't try to think, but forget it as soon as you can. It is dangerous to know too much, and a secret is a burdensome thing. Just think what a narrow escape I had from putting a perfectly innocent woman under suspicion."

He handed the letter back, and bending over her, kissed her, saying : ·

" I have been here an unconscionably long time and must go. When Dr. Sherman returns I will call upon him immediately, and then I hope I can see you daily without remark. Good-by, darling."

He left her, happier than she had been in all her life before.

CHAPTER XXI.

SOME MATTERS OF INTEREST.

THE dread of Dr. Sherman's anger, when he should come to know of her deceit, could not mitigate Lucy's joy. She felt strong now, and a new existence was given her. Not only had love entered her heart and found that welcome a true woman always gives the little god, but she found what she never before had—a staff to lean upon. She now had some one to cling to—to rely upon ; some one to whom she could unburden herself, reserving nothing. It was luxury she had never enjoyed, for there was her secret which she had to guard jealously. Now there was some one she was dear to, who would be interested in her slightest thought, to whom she could freely go with all her troubles. No one had hitherto, except in a brief and a disastrous period, stood in such relation to her, and while Dr. Sherman was kind and generous, still the offense she had committed against him, if not the habitual austerity of his nature, prevented community of sentiment. In short, she had been isolated from that tender human sympathy which is the lot, to the great good fortune of the world, of a vast majority of the young. ·Her experience had been singular and unnatural. That she had passed through the fire of her ordeal without a totally ruinous warping of her moral nature, was strong testimony to the natural goodness of her mind and morals.

Upon Jack's part, it is only due to him to say,

that he had not been blinded by his love for Lucy. He saw without prejudice her fault was grave, amounting in fact to a crime. He was much troubled by it. While his affection for her was by no means diminished, while he was firmly determined he should make her his wife, still he confessed to himself she did not measure up his standard of the ideal woman. But if there was a lessening of the high respect he would have found profound pleasure in according to Mrs. John Gordon, there was a great accession of pity and sympathy for the girl who had been so unfortunate as not to have, at a trying moment of her life, the proper guardians and counselors. He keenly discriminated between the offense itself and the circumstances surrounding the impulse which gave it effect, and he found much to excuse. It was not the commission, as he had said, so much as the continuance of it, over so many years, which was to him so grave. He made up his mind the fault, so far as it could be, should be repaired as quickly as possible, and that he would conduct the reparation so as to shield Lucy as much as she could be shielded from the cousequences of her wrong-doing.

Of course from the standpoint of a rigid moralist this was all wrong. He ought to have spurned with contempt further connection with Lucy, plucked out the love he had conceived for her by the roots, and pluming himself upon the righteousness of his cause, gone straightway to Dr. Sherman and discovered to him the abnormal wickedness of the girl he had cherished and protected, and, with virtuous hugs of himself, looked with melancholy pleasure upon her punishment. But Jack was far too human, had too much of the milk of human kindness in his breast, too much charity in his soul, too great a love for his species and too little for himself; in short, Jack was too much of a Christian to be a rigid moralist.

The days passed by slowly as they waited for the return of Dr. Sherman, who had extended his trip to Washington further south, and thus prolonged his stay from New York. It was, however, a happy time for Lucy, who, basking in the sunshine of her joy, gave no thought of the morrow. She talked, walked, and rode with Jack, content that the glorious days should stretch into eternity. And Jack every day discovered in her some new charm of mind and nature. So it came about that he saw less of his male companions and less of their haunts.

One day he awoke to the fact that he met wherever he went, at whatever hour of the day or night, a person respectably clad, who seemed to have business in whatever part of the city Jack was, and none when he got there. If Jack walked the streets, he was walking in the same direction behind him; if Jack stopped to talk with an acquaintance, the stranger's attention was attracted to the nearest show-window; if Jack went into a hotel, he was there in a moment looking over the news-stand, reading advertisements on the walls, or idly watching passers-by while leaning against a neighboring pillar ; if Jack left his club, by a remarkable coincidence the man was just passing ; if he made a call, while standing at the door waiting for a response to his ring, the man passed by taking note of the number of the house. The only time when he missed him on the street was when he was walking with Lucy.

This had been going on for several days, when the thought occurred to him that the man was a detective dogging his footsteps. This idea had broken upon him as he was walking up Fifth Avenue, opposite the Worth monument, and acting upon the impulse of the moment, he called one of the cabs drawn up at the curbstone, and gave orders to be driven at once to Police Headquarters.

Seeking Captain Lawton, he was at once ushered into that official's room.

" Don't you think," said Jack, "that this persecution of me ought to cease ? "

" What's the matter now ? " calmly queried the Captain.

" I am dogged by one of your hounds every step I take."

The detective smiled, but looked annoyed.

" The fellow has been doing his work badly," he replied. " You should not have known it."

" You confess it then ? "

" Yes. What else could I do ? Be a little reasonable, Mr. Gordon. I have a duty to perform. My profession may not be what comes up to your high notions, but it's work that has got to be done. Now, you've got hold of a clue you won't give up. I've got to get it some way. That's all there is about it. You'd make it easier for me, if you'd tell what you know."

" Well, must an inoffensive private citizen be annoyed in this way ? "

" You don't look at it right, Mr. Gordon," said the detective calmly. " Here's a murder done ; the law says the murderer must be punished. Before that can be done the murderer has got to be caught. That's where we come in. We are in the business because we are necessary to good government. The law don't want to punish a man for revenge ; the law is above revenge ; it punishes severely as a warning that men's lives can't be taken carelessly; it punishes to prevent other murders. Why," said the detective, warming to his subject, and pacing up and down his narrow office, "why what kind of a city would ye have here if anybody could go out and commit a murder for the liking of it—why, with the criminal classes pourin' in here from all parts of the world, if that was allowed, Deadwood, Lead

City, and the mining camps woudn't be a patch on New York. No, sir, you walk to your home after midnight and sleep safe, you go. up and down this city at all hours, safe and unharmed, with more murderers, thieves, sluggers, cutthroats, assassins, and jail-birds in it, than there are people in any of the towns or cities west of Chicago or St. Louis, because we are always tracking crime, and because the prosecuting authorities are always punishing it. Perhaps we don't track crime accordin' to the rules of good society. You are a good deal more intelligent than the ordinary man, Mr. Gordon, and you ought to know that I've got to do my duty without fear or favor. And I want you to know I'm goin' to do it, and I ain't goin' to ask by your leave neither."

Jack could not but recognize the truth of the detective's remarks, and he felt something like admiration for the dogged determination of the man. It quite fell in with his own spirit.

"I believe you are right, Captain," he said, "and I don't think I have looked at the matter or you properly. When a man is doing his duty as he sees it, he is doing the best he can. If I have given you offense in the past, I beg your pardon. Here's my hand."

The detective put out his hand :

"I'd rather any time have you for a friend than an enemy, Mr. Gordon, for you are both a man and a gentleman."

"But," said Jack, "what do you hope to accomplish by shadowing me?"

"I know that a woman committed that murder. You have a suspicion who that woman is—a woman you know. I must, therefore, know all the women you do, and sift them down."

"Well, Captain," said Jack, laughing, "that is too much of a contract for any one man, and I will let you out. The suspicion was all wrong."

"What do you mean?"

"The lady whose good name I was trying to save is not connected with the matter at all."

Jack then told the detective all that had occurred between Mr. and Mrs. Jamieson and himself, suppressing only their names.

"Have you any objections to giving the names of your friends?" said the detective, after a moment's reflection.

"What use would you make of the information? Would you make their names public?"

"Not at all. I have got to search for the last owner or possessor of that pistol. Your friends would serve as a starting-point."

"The people are Mr. and Mrs. Walter Jamieson."

"The swell lawyer of Wall Street? I understand now why you were so careful. It is a thread broken and we're apparently all at sea again. But so much rubbish is cleared away. The point gained is, that it must be some one in the Jamieson set."

"I presume so."

"And you know her."

"Perhaps I do, since I know nearly everybody in that set."

"Exactly. I must go to Jamieson and see if I can not start his memory."

"I do not think you will."

"Why, because he won't try to remember?"

"No, because he can't. He has tried often enough, and is much annoyed over the loss of the pistols. They were rare and valuable."

"I can try," said the detective thoughtfully. "You do not think they went into the hands of Miss Sherman?"

"No, I know that."

"How?"

"Two years ago, when these pistols passed from the hands of Mr. Jamieson, she was in Europe with her father.   Besides, the Jamiesons and she were not acquainted until this winter."

" But they might have gone into her hands indirectly from other people's, recently.   You know she called on Renfrew that day?"

" I know.   So did I.   She visited him before I did.   Renfrew told me so then.   No.   Dismiss that idea.   Now, see here, Captain, I want you to tell me if there is any necessity of bringing Miss Sherman's name in this affair?"

" No, unless she touches the murder or the cause of it."

" She doesn't.   Not even remotely.   I don't mind telling you, Captain, I am. deeply interested in Miss Sherman—that we are engaged, though our engagement is not yet announced."

" And you don't want your bride that is to be mixed up with that fellow's affairs.   That's natural."

" Precisely."

" I suppose she has burnt those letters you got from him?"

" Yes.   But they had no bearing on the murder."

" You told me you didn't know what was in them?"

" I didn't then.   I do now.   I have learned everything from her lips.   The letters were written when she was sixteen or seventeen."

" A foolish flirtation, she said."

" That was a pardonable fib, Captain, to cover the real nature of their contents.   I know the story."

" She may be ' stringing ' you."

Jack was annoyed.

" Now, Captain, I may be a fit subject for 'stringing,' as you call it, but there was none in the case."

" Those letters might have thrown some light on this affair."

" No, they could not have helped you.   But I

will tell you something of value to you, believing that you will not unnecessarily bring her name into the matter."

The detective was interested.

"You have been trying," continued Jack, "to get at Renfrew's antecedents. I will tell you all you can learn after a year's search. His name was Jacob Myers. He changed his name when he adopted the stage as a profession. He had not a single relative on earth except Miss Sherman, who was his cousin."

The detective was deeply interested now.

"Yes," continued Jack. "His family are all dead, and hers also."

"Except Dr. Sherman?"

"No. He is not related to either. Miss Sherman is his adopted daughter. Her name is Annesley."

"Where did he come from?"

"The neighborhood of Cornwall."

"She ought to know something about his life, though?"

"She does not. There never was much intimacy. From the time she was eight until she was seventeen she was continuously at school at Rocky Point. During that time she only saw him at intervals, at the school, when he visited her there. Afterward when she left school and went to Dr. Sherman she saw less of him. He never called on her, and she saw him only on the street. You see, Captain," said Jack, becoming a little more earnest than was necessary, and thereby slightly exciting the suspicion of the detective, "there was a family matter which Miss Sherman had foolishly, even wrongfully, concealed from Dr. Sherman,—a concealment that led to trouble for her and to consequences that were wrong and an outrage upon Dr. Sherman. Of this Myers, or Renfrew, what-

ever you may call him, was aware, and he led her
into a correspondence in which she told under her
own hand the whole story.   With perhaps the most
of men this wouldn't have amounted to much, but
with Dr. Sherman it meant a great deal.   Having got the story in her own handwriting, this
Renfrew began a systematic course of frightening
her ; and she being but a child, and inexperienced,
became alarmed, and instead of going straightway
to the Doctor with it, as she ought to have done,
submitted to blackmail until I stepped in and put
an end to it."

Jack had very adroitly told the story, without
revealing the truth, and he succeeded in lulling the
suspicions of the detective.

" That story," said the Captain, "accounts for
everything I couldn't make connections on.   I see
now why she was so anxious to recover her letters.
No, she hadn't any motive to kill her cousin, for if
the worst had come there would have been a row,
big or little, with the Doctor.   She wouldn't have
been disgraced.   Well, Mr. Gordon, I don't see
any call for the name being roped in."

" I am very glad of that."

" I want to ask you a question, Mr. Gordon.
You saw the woman who called on Renfrew last ? "

" Yes, she came in as I was going out."

" Could you describe her ? "

" No.   She was too closely veiled and dressed
plainly, even poorly, in black.   There was something familiar about her walk and voice, but I
could not fix anything then, and I can't now of
course.   I had an odd idea at the time that she
knew me, for when she saw me descending the
stairs, she walked a step toward me as if she were
about to speak, and then abruptly turned off and
walked away to the boy, who came up at that
moment."

"More proof that she is in your set. That's where I will have to work, Mr. Gordon, I am greatly obliged for this call. You have cleared a deal of brushwood away for me."

The detective turned to his desk, and taking from it a letter handed it to Jack.

"That letter, Mr. Gordon, was written by the woman who killed Renfrew."

Jack took it with some curiosity. It was signed "Dollie Dux," and he recognized the writing to be the same as that in Lucy's possession. The while, the detective watched him keenly as he read it through. Having finished it, he looked at the writing again and at the paper.

"Evidently the letter of an educated woman who is very nice about her stationery," he said, as he handed it back.

"You do not recognize the handwriting?"

"No, I do not."

"What do you mean about the stationery? Anything peculiar?"

"Oh no! It is the stationery of a refined woman, particular about such things. It is hard to explain just what I mean. Show me the letters of a dozen women of various classes and I can pick out the letters of the refined woman of society and breeding from those written by the women who are not."

"Ah," said the detective, feeling that Jack was getting beyond him. "Here are the rest. They may interest you."

Jack took them and looked them over.

"The infamous scamp!" he cried. "How could he treat such a woman so!"

"He was more than infamous," said the detective, in a tone of great disgust. "He was a blind fool. He ought to have known that women who plead that way and don't threaten are far more dangerous in their desperation. Women who have got a high place in society, who are proud, and whose fall is a great fall, nerve themselves up to do the most desperate thing. In my judgment they are driven over the line of insanity. You read those letters and you see that woman hadn't slept for weeks. She was in constant fear of exposure every day. I don't think, when you come right down to it, that she was quite responsible when she did it."

"What makes you fix upon these letters as showing the writer of them murdered Renfrew?" asked Jack.

"The way she talked in them first gave me the idea. Then I concluded, as you did, that she was well up in society and had a great deal to lose in exposure. But when I compared the dates, I found she was the only one he was having an affair with at the time. All the others were finished. See," he continued, showing Jack another package. "He indorses on the back, 'Played out to end.' 'No further good.' He had some such indorsement on all the rest."

"Do you suppose she went there with deliberate intent to kill?"

"That is hard to tell. You don't know what her intent was. Doubtless her motives were mixed. If the truth could only be known I believe she hadn't any fixed plan. No doubt she had an idea of killing somebody, since she had a loaded pistol with her, but it might have been herself she thought of doing. Then something occurred between them, and on the impulse she killed him."

"Do you think that stationery—that kind—was used by her only?" he continued.

"No," replied Jack, "probably two hundred women in New York are using the same kind to-day."

"You see there is a scent of patchouli on them,"

said the detective. " The pistol had it too when I first found it."

" That might prove to be a clue," said Jack. " I don't think women of society use that kind of perfume much. If they do they don't confine themselves to one kind."

" That is a point to know," replied the detective. " Well, Mr. Gordon, the man who has been annoying you by following you, shall be withdrawn immediately."

" Thanks."

They shook hands on parting, having a hearty respect for each other.

CHAPTER XXII.

TRUE LOVE RUNS SMOOTHLY.

A DAY or two after the second interview between Captain Lawton and Jack, the latter received information that Dr. Sherman was at home. Accordingly he addressed a polite note to that gentleman, requesting permission to call upon a matter of importance, at any hour that day which might be named by the Doctor.

In due course of time his messenger returned with the word that the Doctor had appointed the hour of four. As his business with Dr. Sherman was momentous and demanded proper preparation, Jack determined that he would not go out until the approach of the hour he was to call upon Lucy's father. So he spent the day in framing speeches until the time for dressing, when making an elaborate toilet he sallied forth.

On his way he met " Dizzy " Lowell and Will Robb, come in search of him with a desire to carry him off to some sport they had in hand.

"Where have you kept yourself?" cried Robb. " The town languishes for you, and your friends know you not."

"Yes," chimed in " Dizzy," "you've bolted the course."

" Having become implicated in a murder affair," said Jack in reply, " it behooves me to keep quiet."

" Oh, pshaw ! " said " Dizzy." " We pulled you through that all right. You don't want to get out of training because of that little thing, do you ? "

"The truth is," replied Jack, anxious to be rid of them, "I have had a great many things pressing on me because of that complication, all of which you shall know in good time."

"Well, all right," said Robb,—"but we have got up a private scrapping match. We want you to go with us this afternoon."

"Impossible. I have an engagement."

"With a woman? Throw it over."

"No, it's not a woman and I can't throw it over."

"Hope it's not more of that Renfrew case," said "Dizzy" anxiously. "'Tain't 'nother arrest, is it?"

"Worse, far worse," said Jack solemnly; "may involve my liberty for my whole life. But I must be off. Good-by, old chappies."

And before they could detain him he had turned the corner.

The two looked at each other in alarm.

"Jack's going to the bad," said "Dizzy" mournfully.

"Tell you what it is," said Robb earnestly, as a new thought broke on him. "He's going to propose to some woman. He's going to get married."

"Oh, the devil! Not so bad as that. Hang it, that's worse than the other. Can't we do something to pull him through?"

"Who is the woman, I wonder?"

"Damfino! Wish it was my sister. She wants just such a cool head and light hand on the mouth. She's a good girl, too, with all her nonsense, and I'll bet she'll trot better double than single."

Will, having inclinations in the direction suggested by his friend, could not echo the wish, though he indorsed the sentiment.

In the mean time Jack was making his way to the B——— hotel. He had informed Lucy by note that he should call on the Doctor to make a formal demand for her hand that day at four, and so, when he was ushered into the presence of her father, she was not present.

The Doctor gave him a courteous greeting—indeed a cordial one. Jack argued therefrom a satisfactory result for his call. He was wrong, however, in his supposition, for it is to be doubted whether the Doctor had given a moment's thought to the object of Jack's visit. But it happened he had traveled from Washington the day previous with Mr. Van Huyn, who had entertained him with an account of Jack's confinement, and his refusal to involve a lady's name in a scandal on mere suspicion, even if the result were to him confinement in jail, and the old gentleman, thinking it an evidence of fine and chivalric feeling, was highly prepossessed in Jack's favor.

Jack opened his business without delay.

" Doctor," he said, "the object of my call is to propose in this formal manner for the hand of your daughter."

The old gentleman was startled. The marriage of Lucy was something he had not contemplated as likely to occur in the immediate future at least. Jack's blunt proposition disconcerted him.

He fidgeted about in his chair for a moment or two, looking somewhat irritably upon the calm, elegant figure before him.

"Why, Mr. Gordon," he at length said, "your proposal startles me ! I have had no reason to anticipate the honor, and—and—indeed I have not thought of Miss Sherman's marriage."

" I beg, sir," said Jack, in his most deferential manner, "you will give it consideration, and," he added insinuatingly, " favorable consideration."

" I presume," said the old gentleman, "you have the young lady's permission to address me ? "

Jack answered him that he had, adding that else

he would not have taken it upon himself to seek such an interview.

"In my young days it was thought necessary to ask the parent for permission to address the daughter. But the world moves along and we old people find ourselves left behind, unable to keep up with the rapid motion of the present. Whether it is an improvement I doubt. However, I shall not endeavor to stop the way with my feeble protest. I confess to you that my idea was that Miss Sherman should not marry before twenty-five. She is twenty-two now."

"If you will permit me," said Jack, "before we go further into this conversation, I will make a statement concerning myself which you ought to have, and which you would naturally expect me to make, if you were to look favorably upon my suit."

"The young dog expresses himself well," thought the old man.

"I desire to say," continued Jack, "that I am well born, and have an ample fortune to maintain my wife in all the comfort and luxury she has been accustomed to ; that I am well educated ; refined I hope, and that my morals are certainly not worse than the average young man of the day."

"Indeed, Mr. Gordon," said the Doctor, "I have heard nothing of you that is not admirable. And I distinctly wish you to understand that I do not resent your proposition. It is a high compliment to a lady when a man so distinguishes her from among her sex. I so regard your proposition. There are several things, however, I desire to say. Are you aware that Miss Sherman is not my daughter, that she bears my name by adoption only ?"

"The lady has so informed me."

"Very properly under the circumstances," said the old gentleman. "Did she tell you why I adopted her ?"

"She was not explicit. I think, if I understood her rightly, because of the great regard you bore the memory of her father."

This was adroit of Jack, and he saw the old man was greatly pleased.

"You misunderstood her, sir," he replied ; "it was the mother. Are you aware that Miss Sherman has no fortune of her own ?"

"I have not given the matter a second's thought. I care not whether she has one or two pennies. I have, thanks to my father, far more than enough for both."

The old gentleman was pleased again. Jack was doing famously.

"Well, Mr. Gordon, I confess I do not look upon the loss of Miss Sherman with favor. She has grown dear to me, and what is perhaps more to a selfish old man, rather necessary to my old age."

"It will not, I am sure, be a total loss, though her affections may be divided."

"If what you have told me is true, I fear the division has already taken place. However, I can not expect to dam the current of young people's affections, and I have no right to deprive Lucy of her proper and natural life. But have you not been somewhat precipitate in your action ?"

"I think not, sir. I will tell you frankly I have not known the moment since I first saw her that I have not loved her deeply."

"Ah, yes, at Mrs. Jamieson's. I thought then you were greatly attracted to each other." The old man laughed. "I warned her against your specious tongue, but the warning seems to have had no effect."

To this Jack made no reply.

"Well," continued the Doctor, "I have no objections to present, Mr. Gordon. If I refrain from giving my sanction at this moment, it is only because I desire to satisfy myself that Miss Sherman's affections are truly engaged, and because in my duty to her I wish to make the proper inquiries as to yourself. I have no doubt everything is as you say, and being so I will not withhold my sanction. Sir, I congratulate you on having won the affections of a very fine woman."

The blood rushed into the face of Jack on this remark, for he thought of the interview he must subsequently have with this fine, honorable old gentleman, and the revelation he would have to make. He felt a profound pity for him. However, he rose, and taking the old man's hand he shook it warmly, and said :

" I thank you, sir ; I am not unappreciative of my good fortune. I hope if your inquiries result to my favor you will find in my love, care, and protection of your daughter, reason to conclude that you have acted wisely in confiding her to me."

He hesitated a moment, still holding the old man's hand, and then went on, his voice trembling a bit: " And I venture to hope you will find, so far from having lost a daughter, you have gained a son, and that I shall have replaced the father I lost so early."

The old man was not a little moved by this unexpected outburst of Jack, and he returned the shake of his hand heartily.

There was so much in common in the natures of both that, having had a glimpse of the heart of the other, they had come to fancy each other greatly, and both were sincere. But what had touched Jack most keenly was the pity he felt for Dr. Sherman, when he should know how he had been deceived.

Jack soon after took his leave.

" A fine fellow. A fine, manly, wholesome young

fellow," said the Doctor, as he paced up and down the room with his hands behind his back.

"He is an old trump. A fine, courtly old gentleman. He's a brick," said Jack, as he descended the stairs.

The Doctor was still pacing up and down the room in the darkening shadows when Lucy came in.

"So," said the Doctor, facing about upon her with pretended severity.—"So, I can not leave town for a short time but you must begin to make love to one of the rapid young men of the town!"

"Mr. Gordon is not rapid, he is a very noble man," said Lucy, blushing, and quick to resent any aspersion upon Jack.

"Now, did I say anything about Mr. Gordon?" asked the Doctor, struggling hard to repress the smile on his lips, and very much pleased with her quick defense. "There are young men in New York other than Mr. Gordon, I presume."

Lucy, realizing her blunder, colored deeply and made no reply.

"So, so! It is Mr. Gordon who has been trifling with your affections, is it? I warned you against that young man when you first met him."

Lucy walked up to him that she might see his expression, looking anxiously into his face.

He took her hand in his own and patting it kindly said:

"So there is somebody in this world who wishes to own and possess for himself this pretty little hand. Tell me, my dear, do you love him,—this Mr. Gordon?"

Lucy hung her head with becoming modesty, and acknowledged she did.

"Are you certain it is not a mere passing fancy for an elegant young man who knows how to make himself agreeable?"

"No, father," she said, "I love him with all my

heart. He is not merely an elegant young man. He is a noble, high-minded, generous gentleman, worthy to be mated to the best lady in the land— much my superior. I not only love him ; I adore him. I am humbled by his love for me."

The old man drew her to him and kissed her on the forehead.

"I am satisfied on that point," he said ; "I agree with you, he is a fine fellow, a fine, manly, wholesome young fellow. I am sorry to lose you, Lucy. You have been a good daughter to me. But if I am to do so, as I suppose I must some time, it is to such a man I wish to give you. If all I hear of this young robber is borne out, I shall sanction your engagement. But hurry away, my dear, and prepare for the evening. Young folks may live on love, but old ones must dine."

And Lucy did hasten away, for she was con- science-stricken because of his kindness, and remorse-stricken over her deceit.

CHAPTER XXIII.

A WOLF AMONG THE LAMBS.

THE two young people were not left long in doubt as to the sanction of Dr. Sherman. His inquiries were speedily made and apparently satisfactory. Lucy early informed Mrs. Van Huyn of her engagement, and Jack did not delay in carrying to Mrs. Jamieson, his steadfast friend, the all-important fact.

"It is all very provoking, Jack," said that lady. "I intended selecting your wife myself, and here you have chosen and not even consulted me. I don't know that I should have done any better, certainly not in appearances, for you will have a lovely bride. But after I have been carefully training you in the way you should go for so many years, to find that you go off in this independent manner is very discouraging. Not that I have a word to say against your love. Oh, no! But I must be propitiated. You must let me give a party next week at which your engagement is to be announced. I insist upon it."

"I will consent," replied Jack laughing, "if Lucy will. And I imagine she will not object. I may have to ask favors of you before the honeymoon is reached, so I shall be very obedient."

Lucy's consent was easily secured, and the "world went very well in those days." The only thing occurring to occasionally dim Lucy's happiness and to cause Jack grave apprehension, was the thought of the necessity of informing Dr. Sherman of Lucy's deceit. Jack insisted that the doctor must be told, and Lucy yielded always, though she found excuses for the postponement of the revelation. The only question was, when it should be, done. Jack determined that the best results would be obtained after the announcement of their engagement, and after Dr. Sherman had given public sanction thereto.

Mr. Jamieson's party occurred the following week; the surprise she had promised her friends was complete. Jack was the recipient of the warmest congratulations from the men and Lucy was prouder than ever of her lover, for she felt she was greatly envied by more than one young lady present.

Mollie Lowell and Lou Appleby came to her together, saying :

" We do not propose to forgive you as long as you live, Miss Sherman. Your offense is beyond forgiveness. Jack belongs to us by right of long expectancy."

" Not to both of you, I hope," replied Lucy, laughing.

" Yes, to both of us," said Mollie. " He has made love to us both ever since he was ten years old, and indeed in this very room, on the very first night he met you, he held out inducements to us, if we would behave ourselves he would marry us both. Didn't he, Lou ?"

" You impeach his morals ! " cried Lucy.

" He did indeed, Miss Sherman," said Lou Appleby, " But we didn't behave ourselves because we can't. It's all very unfair. You don't know what you have done—what misery you have caused. My l my ! how we will all be scolded tonight. The great eligible is gone."

" Hook, bob, and sinker, as ' Dizzy ' says," interrupted Mollie.

"All of us have been trained from our youth upward," continued Miss Appleby, "to ensnare this same Jack Gordon ; all our education has been to that end, and just think of the rage of all managing mammas over the failure of the dear daughters. You have no consideration, Miss Sherman. You have no right to be so beautiful and charming."

"Yes, and that is not the worst of it," added Mollie. "How are we to get our extra gowns and the rest of the things now ? The hint that Mr. Gordon was very tender the last time we met, and the suggestion that a new toilette would fetch him at the next, was sufficient in the past. But, and again I quote my brother, 'that little racket won't work any more.'"

"You perceive the widespread ruin you have caused," said Lou Appleby. "I have grave doubts now if anybody will marry me. Jack's promise was the nearest approach I ever had to an offer."

"Take 'Dizzy,'" said Mollie ; "I'll give him to you."

"I should have to wrap myself in a horse-blanket and put a bridle on my head before he would even think to look at me."

Lucy laughed heartily over the whimsical speech, recognizing its point, through Jack's description of "Dizzy's" devotion to the stable.

"Miss Sherman," said Mollie, dropping into a seat beside Lucy, "while we joke we congratulate you. Jack and I were neighbors when we were children and have always been friends—chums. He is a sterling good fellow, a trusty, true gentleman."

Lucy thanked her so heartily with her eyes, bending toward her, that Mollie thought she was about to kiss her in the crowded rooms.

"Oh, don't kiss me!" she cried, "you'll get paint

on your lips. I'm only kissable in the morning. It's a way I have of keeping the men off."

Lucy looked so horrified, that Lou Appleby, noticing it, said :

"Nonsense ! There never was any paint on that blooming cheek. There ! " and bending over her friend she kissed her.

Will Robb at this moment joined the group.

"The ease and indifference with which you perform that solemn and much to-be-desired rite," said he to Miss Appleby, "is particularly harrowing to my soul."

"Never mind about the much-desired rite, Will," said Mollie, "congratulate Miss Sherman."

"I can't do it, Miss Sherman. Upon my word I can't. I have performed the ceremony with Jack. He is to be congratulated. But you are stealing him from us you see."

"Why, Will, that is quite a pretty speech," said Miss Appleby.

"Yes, Will is improving," chimed in Mollie, "about the time I am ready to accept him, he will do to propose."

"About what time will that time be ? " said Will taking out his watch.

"Oh dear, this is too bad," cried Miss Appleby. "Bring me a horse-blanket and a bridle and send for ' Dizzy.' "

"Dizzy," however, was not taking the news as cheerfully as the rest. He had gone to Jack as soon as he had seen him, and with anxious solicitude had said :

"I say, Jack, can't anything be done to get you out of this scrape ? "

Jack, who was very fond of " Dizzy," and knew what a loyal heart beat under all his peculiarities, laughed heartily and said :

"Oh, no, you don't, 'Dizzy.' I have tried too hard to get into it, to try now to get out of it."

"Dizzy" looked at him sorrowfully.

"Another good 'un gone."

"Come," said Jack, "don't draw so mournful a face. Let me present you to the fair mistress of my heart."

Slipping his arm through that of "Dizzy," he led him to where Lucy was sitting, surrounded by his friends.

"Lucy," he said, "let me present one of my dearest friends, who is trying to persuade me that I have made an irretrievable mistake."

"Ah, come now, Jack!" said "Dizzy," becoming pink to the tip ends of his ears. "That is not at all fair, you know. If he must marry, Miss Sherman, he couldn't do better, you know."

A burst of laughter greeted his speech, in which Jack joined, and which Lucy did not take in good part.

"You see, Miss Sherman," said "Dizzy," much disconcerted, "they're all laughing at me. They always do. It is because I'm such a duffer with my tongue. But what I mean is, that I am Jack's friend, and if he is glad, then I'm glad. And I know when I look at you that he's a devilish lucky fellow, and if you're going to be Jack's wife, then you've got me for a friend."

"Bravo, 'Dizzy,'" cried Will.

"So say we all," said Lou.

Lucy fully comprehended "Dizzy" now, and, smiling, with eyes in which there was suspicious moisture, she put out her hand and grasped "Dizzy's" warmly.

"I accept the friendship, Mr. Lowell."

"I am not Mr. Lowell," said that gentleman, feeling he had recovered himself right well. "That's Mr. Lowell," pointing to his sister. "She's got the head, if it is full of nonsense. I'm 'Dizzy' to you."

"And to every one else," said that young lady. "You've done well, 'Dizzy,' as you usually do in the end. Now, don't say any more, or you will spoil it all."

"Miss Sherman," said Miss Appleby, "you have around you all of Jack's most intimate friends who are still unmarried. We hope you'll take us all in, too."

"Still unmarried," said Will Robb, mischievously. "That reminds me, 'Dizzy,' just before you came up, Lou was saying she was going to make a dead set at you."

"Well, Lou ain't so bad," said "Dizzy," looking at her. "A fellow might do worse."

"Thank you, 'Dizzy,'" said Lou, mischievously, after the laugh had subsided. "Am I to take that as a proposal in form?"

"Oh, hang it, no!" cried "Dizzy" quickly. "You can't stable me that way."

"Another chance gone, Lou," cried Mollie, amid the laughter. "'Two old maids we be.'"

By this time "Dizzy" was pulling Jack aside by the arms.

"I say, Jack, I've just tumbled. That's the woman we bet about, the one you drove in a cab."

"You're right, 'Dizzy,'" said Jack, "but, for Heaven's sake, don't say anything about it now."

"Oh, I'm mum, if you want it so," said "Dizzy." "Talking about 'mum,' let's go and get some 'fizz.' It's awful dry work doing the polite."

Thus it was that the engagement was announced, and there followed this party a round of receptions and dinners that nearly wore out poor Dr. Sherman, who seemed to think it incumbent to attend all and manifest his pride in Lucy's prospective husband.

It was at one of these receptions following the party given by Mrs. Jamieson, that Jack, while wandering about, saw before him the figure of a man, strangely out of place and yet familiar to him. To his intense surprise, and also to his displeasure, he discovered in the person Captain Lawton.

"I suppose you are much astonished to find me here?" said the Captain.

"I confess it—"

"Well, it is somewhat astonishing, I suppose. But you ought to know it is a very common thing in New York society to have a police officer at parties and receptions now in full dress."

"So much the worse for New York society—I did not know it."

"I am surprised at that. However, it is not my line of duty, though I am following it up pretty sharp now."

"Oh, I understand," said Jack, a light breaking in upon him.

"Yes," replied the Captain, "and I am getting closer and closer to the end."

"Have you fixed upon the person?" said Jack, much interested.

"No. But it's one of seven. It was one of eight yesterday. I'll work it down to the one. I'm on the right track now, thanks to you."

This remark did not please Jack, for he felt as if the Captain was taking him into partnership in a business for which he had a peculiar loathing. And bidding him a short good-by, he left him and sought another room.

CHAPTER XXIV.

STARTLING NEWS.

HOWEVER easy the task of revealing the story of Lucy's deceit to Dr. Sherman may have appeared, Jack found, as the time he had fixed upon approached, it grew more difficult and dis-agreeable. How was he to palliate Lucy's offense to this gentleman of high honor and rigid propriety, with his strict notions as to the relations of man to man and to society? This was the problem always present, and it is not surprising if at times he be-came faint-hearted, and was inclined to let every-thing go—to let·matters take their own course. Lucy, perceiving Jack to be more grave and pre-occupied than was his wont, and fearing, now that the first novelty of his love was worn off, he was regretting his alliance with one who had such a stain upon her, was very unhappy. However, she was greatly mistaken. If anything Jack was fonder of her than the day he declared his love. Though perplexed and often grave with apprehension, he was really feeling that now he had her to think for, to care for, his life was fuller, sweeter, and more interesting.

While thus disturbed by doubts and perplexities, Jack further troubled her by insisting upon an early marriage ; that it should take place before Lent. Lucy rebelled. She pointed out to him that six weeks had not elapsed since they had be-come acquainted—that such precipitation would give the world a great deal to talk about. What the world would or would not think Jack cared little, and as to the brief period of their acquaintance and courtship, he replied, that their case was singular and not to be measured by the experience of others. Peculiar circumstances surrounded their acquaintance; they had been drawn closer together, had been enabled to peer more deeply into each other's heart and nature, than would, under other conditions, have fallen to their lot in a year's intimacy. Lucy, who had early fallen into the habit of being guided by Jack, yielded, though without being convinced of the wisdom of the course proposed by her lover.

However, Jack had looked more deeply into their affairs than she. With her he apprehended such severe displeasure upon the part of Dr. Sherman, that he feared she would be without a home, and he felt he must be prepared to give her one as soon as possible. So an early marriage was settled upon.

Ever since Jack had assumed the relations of a prospective son-in-law to the Sherman household, it had been his custom to almost daily entice the Doctor out for a walk. The two had become fond of each other. Jack had the greatest respect for the Doctor, who had seen much of the world. The old man with his great stores of information, which, embellished by a lively fancy, shrewd observation, and dry wit, he poured forth under Jack's genial influence and intelligent appreciation, made him a delightful and entertaining companion for the younger man.

On the occasion of one of these walks, Jack had deftly led the way in the direction of his own apartments, and on reaching the house said:

" Doctor, here is the house in which I live. I take it these houses were not unknown to you abroad, but they are comparatively an innovation in New York. They are houses, you know, designed for the occupation of bachelors. I think, though I may be mistaken, they are more elegant and commodious than anything known abroad. Won't you step in and see how I am housed ?"

The Doctor complied. In this Jack had a purpose. He felt he would be at an advantage in the revelation he was to make, if he were the host rather than the guest. They had been talking of the discovery of a defalcation by a man who moved in good society, who had been greatly trusted, and who was known to both—who had died before the discovery was made.

After the apartments had been duly admired and their convenience praised, and while seated in the parlor, the Doctor renewed the conversation by saying :

" After all, in the case of poor Dillingworth, whether there was crime depends largely upon the intent. So far as I can learn there does not seem to be any property left to his family, and the indications are that he used funds of one trust to make up deficiencies in others. Was he using these funds for speculation for his own benefit ? Or was he hoping thus to repair damages he had made in others by poor investments—to cover up errors of judgment. It is largely a question of intent. I think that all fault should be measured by intent, and to a great degree by the amount of and the kind of intelligence which surrounds or influences its commission. What would be a crime in one of intelligence, intellectuality, and experience in affairs might in another, not possessing such attributes, be a venial fault."

" The Doctor has opened the way," thought Jack, " in an almost providential manner."

" Of course," continued the Doctor, " I don't suppose the law can with propriety make so close

a distinction, but men in their judgments can. We
do as between children and adults."

"Yes, sir," replied Jack. "I know of a case
which illustrates your point. A young girl, a mere
child in fact, standing alone without friends or
proper counselors, urged by a false friend much
older than herself, not appreciating fully the consequences of her act, actually perpetrated a fraud
upon one who came to her as a generous benefactor."

"The child's crime should be measured in such
a case by her intelligence and moral responsibility."

"The peculiarity of this case," continued Jack,
"was that the benefactor was offering her kindness and protection, when he thought he was offering it to another person."   ·

"It was then a case of false pretense?"

"Entirely so."

"One may get into a maze of metaphysics in an
attempt to analyze, subdivide, and classify crime
and intent, and the discussion become intermin-
able. But there are degrees of crime that may be
easily stated. False pretense is a lie with a serious
intent. And a lie is a crime or a fault for which
there is the least excuse. The lowest intelligence
can differentiate truth and falsehood, and the most
blunted moral nature can appreciate the wrong of
falsehood. Now, in the case you speak of, the
degree of the grievousness of this false pretense
depends upon the motive. Let me illustrate.
These apartments might not be yours; they might
belong to a friend; but possessing yourself of their
keys, you might, as you have done this morning,
invite me to them, pretending they were yours,
having for your motive only the idea I would consider you of more importance if I thought you
possessed such elegant rooms. Your false pretense
would have done me no harm, and you would have

only gratified a silly vanity. But if it had been done for the purpose of impressing me with an idea of your wealth and station, when you had none, to induce me for instance to grant you the hand of my daughter, you would have committed a crime. So in the case you speak of. What was to be accomplished by her false pretense?"

"A home, care, protection, freedom from the curse of poverty."

"Ah, that is bad. You say the benefactor supposed her to be some one else?"

"Yes. He came to the school searching for another of the same name, and was misled by others into supposing this girl to be the one he sought. She was but a little over sixteen—nearly seventeen, in fact."

As he said this, Jack bent a piercing glance upon the old gentleman. The words and the glance aroused the Doctor. He looked steadily into Jack's eyes for a long time, and Jack as steadily returned the look. Ideas were communicated in these glances.

"You have a purpose in telling me this case, Mr. Gordon," said the Doctor sternly.

"I have," replied Jack, "and no one can grieve more than I that I have a story to tell you."

"And it relates to—" inquired the old man, his face becoming white with apprehension.

"To Lucy."

"My God!" cried the old Doctor, sinking back in his chair and dropping his head on his breast.

No words were spoken by either for some time. Jack watched the expressions chasing each other over the face of the fine old gentleman sitting overwhelmed before him. Perceiving the Doctor had recovered from the first shock, he proceeded with the story. He told it with all the art he was capable of. He dwelt upon Lucy's homeless and friendless condition ; her lack of home training and moral guidance ; of her deprivation of a mother's care and influence ; on the wicked cousin, with his specious counsel and malign influence ; how Lucy had begun the correspondence with the Doctor in good faith, and only continued it under the urgency of this Mephistopheles. He showed Lucy's struggles with herself and her gradual slipping into the crime ; the aid the Doctor gave her unconsciously; the conspiracy of events, all tending to force her into her false position. He pictured her fear of the Doctor, her fear to reveal her wickedness afterward, her penitence, her unhappiness, and the tortures she had been subjected to by Renfrew. Then he artfully presented her charming qualities, her affection for the Doctor, the obedience she had given him, her devotion, and the brightness and interest she had brought into his life.

Then he waited to see the effect he had produced. The old man did not look up for a long time, and the lines grew deeper in his face. After a long period of thought he said :

"You plead her cause well and eloquently, but it is useless, John," for such he had come to call him.

Jack made no reply ; he had none to make.

"She has trifled with the most sacred sentiment of my heart."

"That, sir," said Jack, "is a refinement she could not have been expected at her age to have appreciated."

"She has practiced fraud, deceit, and misrepresentation for five years—her life has been a living lie."

"The act was committed five years ago, and the rest was a consequence."

"Do not seek longer to defend her. I am crushed by this revelation. To think I should have been a dupe of such a wicked, designing chit—a wicked fraud—a s—"

"Stop, please, sir, before you apply an epithet you will afterward regret," said Jack, gently, laying his own upon the hand of the old man.

The touch seemed to check the rising passion of the Doctor.

"Well," he said, "I'll pluck her from my heart. She had won her way and wound herself tightly about it. I cast her off. John, we'll both forget her, and perhaps because of our sorrows be closer together."

"Pardon me," said Jack firmly, "I'll not forget her. She is my promised bride—my chosen wife. I shall marry her."

"Are you mad, boy?" said the old man angrily. "You propose to marry this advent—"

"Stop, sir," thundered Jack. "I'll not listen to abuse of her. She is my wife now in the sight of God, and no man, no matter what his wrongs may be, shall say one word against the wife of John Gordon."

Headstrong and unaccustomed to opposition as was the Doctor, he nevertheless looked with admiration upon the figure Jack presented.

"My lad," he said, "you propose to marry her still? Don't you know that I have a duty to perform, in punishing her? She must be imprisoned for her crime."

"Yes, I shall marry her," replied Jack firmly, "even if I have to go behind prison bars to do it, Doctor. I love her, and love with me is not an idle thing. Sir, since we have become acquainted I have grown very fond of you. I believe you have of me. You have so treated me."

The old man nodded his head in acquiescence.

"I have been grateful to you for your favor, and have been proud of it, and I do not believe that you will do that which will cause me sorrow, shame, and humiliation. I am to be considered in this matter. It is my affair, as well as Lucy's and yours."

"But how can you marry one for whom you must have lost your respect? Why, my lad, if she has deceived me in this manner, she would deceive her husband."

"No, sir, I can not believe it," returned Jack earnestly. "I have seen into her heart. I know how penitent she is. I know how she has been purified by the fire she has gone through. She has suffered, and through suffering she is regenerated. Lucy Sherman is not the Lucy Annesley you found. Do not take offense if I say I have read that girl more deeply than you. When she came to me that day in the jail, trembling with the fear I was suffering confinement through my efforts to save her; offering to reveal to you the deception she had practiced, in the belief that it would release me; earnestly proposing to sacrifice herself that I might be free; confessing her love for me, yet refusing to accept mine because of the bar she had erected by her misdeed, the stain she had put upon herself, she made expiation. And in that act of generous abnegation she showed herself to be what she is, a penitent woman—purified by sacrifice—a tender, loving, fine woman. It is nothing that I loved her the more for it. It is nothing that I refused to accept her *dictum*. It is nothing that when she told me her story to end my love for her, I took her in my arms and vowed before the God who is the Judge of us all that I would love and cherish her forever in my heart of hearts, come what there might to her. I shall marry her, sir, proud and happy to do it, and I ask you if it is your purpose to strike at John Gordon through his wife?"

"God forgive me, I can't," cried the old man, his eyes glistening with the tears in them, his face quivering with admiration for the loyal and devoted young man, strong in his love and enthusiasm. "I won't do it. But between her and me all is at an end. Take her away, John, take her away. I do not want to see her again. And she was so dear to me! She seemed to make green and pleasant my barren old age. But take her away, John. I will wait here until she has removed herself. I can not go back and look at her again. Take her away, John."

He rose and walked to the window to signify all further discussion was at an end.

Jack stood where the Doctor had left him, thinking profoundly for a long time, and then he said :

"I will do as you wish, Doctor. I will take her away. Please remain here until I return."

He hastened out and made his way quickly to Mrs. Van Huyn. He told this lady that a difference, and he feared an irreparable one, had arisen between Dr. Sherman and Lucy, and he wanted her to take care of her for a few days, until arrangements could be made for her. He assured her that neither she nor Mr. Van Huyn would incur the enmity of the Doctor in so doing, and that he pledged himself to reconcile Mr. Van Huyn to Lucy's coming into the house.

To this Mrs. Van Huyn gave cheerful, indeed, eager compliance, saying she was ready to receive Lucy at any moment. Jack, therefore, hurried off to accomplish Lucy's removal, which was soon done, and before the night the Doctor returned to the empty rooms feeling himself to be a very lonely, forlorn old man as he dined alone.

CHAPTER XXV.

EVENTS PROGRESS RAPIDLY.

IT was to be supposed that the fact of an irreparable quarrel between Lucy and her father, occurring so closely after her engagement to Jack, would have caused a great deal of gossip. There was much speculation as to its cause. The Doctor maintained a discreet silence, and of course Jack and Lucy did not make explanations. Mrs. Van Huyn maintained silence for the best of reasons, she didn't know. For though she had given shelter to Lucy gladly, she did not receive confidence in return. To Mr. Van Huyn Jack had said that the unfortunate difference was wholly a family matter, in which he, Jack, occupied a singularly contradictory position. While he could not blame Dr. Sherman, who certainly had a right to form what judgment he chose, and to govern himself and household as he saw fit, still he, Jack, sustained Lucy to the utmost.

Mr. Van Huyn, who knew the Doctor well, and knew how firm he was in having his own way, even inclined to use force to accomplish his ends, thought, though Jack had not intended that impression to be made, that the Doctor had laid a command upon Lucy relative to her engagement with Jack with which she refused to comply ; that the alternative of complying or leaving the Doctor having been presented she accepted the latter.

That the difference had arisen over the engagement was the unanimously accepted version. Indeed, it went to the point of the alleged discovery of some peccadillos of Jack, one of which lived in a cross-street where her bills were paid by Jack, and who was far too pretty to be countenanced by virtuous women. But as Jack was extremely popular, and as all this gossip contributed to turning what otherwise would have been only an ordinary engagement into a romance, the world sided with Jack and Lucy, and heartily condemned the old Doctor, who, as "Dizzy" Lowell, true to his friend, had said in the club one night, "dropped the flag on the youngsters before they had a fair start."

It was fortunate for both that a woman of the standing of Mrs. Van Huyn had thrown the mantle of her partisanship over Lucy by receiving her in her house. Mrs. Jamieson, profoundly grateful to Jack, and inspired by her husband, settled everything for them in the world of fashion, by giving a most distinguished dinner-party at which Jack and Lucy were honored guests. All things, therefore, were moving smoothly.

Jack knew, however, that affairs could not go on indefinitely in this manner, and so after many consultations, in which the wise heads of their friends Madames Van Huyn and Jamieson were employed, the date, and an early one, not three weeks away, was fixed for the wedding.

This became all the more necessary, in Jack's opinion, for the reason that Mr. Van Huyn was compelled to go to Europe in a short time, and though his wife was disinclined to accompany him, was strongly urging her to do so. True, Mrs. Jamieson offered a way out of this difficulty by proposing shelter for Lucy under her roof, but Jack was not satisfied to have Lucy shunted from one house to another. There was only one course to pursue in his judgment, and that, an early marriage. In the end all came to his way of thinking.

Jack now spent a great deal of his time at Mrs. Van Huyn's house. That lady **was** as gracious as could be desired. She laughingly said she had told Lucy, the day after she first met Jack, that there would be a romance, and that she (Mrs. Van Huyn) would be called upon to preside over it. As her prediction had been verified, she would do it in the most approved manner.

Mr. Van Huyn's mansion was a large, roomy house of the extreme modern style on Madison Avenue, on a corner. At the rear of the hall in the center of the house, and between the dining-room on one side and a conservatory on the other, both of which were extensions from the main build-ing, was a small, cosey room, which Mrs. Van Huyn had taken as her own private and special apart-ment. She called it her office, for there she attended to her household accounts and consulted her ser-vants. After Lucy had come into the house, she had said to Lucy and Jack that she would give up that room to them in the afternoons, for there they would be free from callers or interruption of any kind.

And in this room one afternoon, ten days or more after the separation of Lucy and Dr. Sher-man, we find Jack and Lucy. He had already obtained possession of a house, and was hastening the preparations for their occupancy immediately after their return from their retirement following the ceremonies. He had been telling her, with a great deal of enthusiasm, of Mrs. Jamieson's prep-arations for the reception, which that warm-hearted lady had determined should take place at her house, and was now describing to her the arrangement of the rooms of their new home.

They were thus pleasantly engaged, when a card was brought to Jack by one of the servants. To his great surprise he read the name of Captain

Lawton. Somewhat startled by this disagreeable reminder of past events, he asked the servant where his visitor was.

" In the reception-room," was the answer.

On going there, he found the Captain standing in the middle of the room, from which point he could command a view of the adjoining apartments.

" I suppose you are surprised and not very well pleased to have me follow you here," said the Captain, " but I have been trying to see you for several days, and as I couldn't see you without coming here, why I had to come, that's all."

" Take a seat, Captain," said Jack in reply. " What's up now ? "

Drawing a chair into the middle of the room the Captain sat down.

" You know when I last saw you," he replied, " I told you I had figured it down to seven. Now, as you are a master hand at cleaning off brushwood, I thought, perhaps, you would give me some further assistance."

" You know," said Jack, " I don't like to be engaged in this sort of thing. I hoped I should be free from it all by this time."

" I know, Mr. Gordon, that you don't like it," replied the Captain, " but this isn't asking you to detect anybody. I've got seven on my hands now and the whole of them bother me. Don't you see ? There are some suspicious circumstances that point to two persons. I don't exactly believe they are into it, or that they even knew Renfrew. But the circumstances exist, and so long as they do, and I don't know something to the contrary, why I have got to take them into consideration, and they bother me."

" I see. How can I help you ? "

" They are two friends of yours."

" Oh ! Well, what then ? "

"Well, if I could get a sight of their handwriting I might know whether there was any use of counting them in."

"Who are these ladies?"

"Miss Mary Lowell and Miss Louise Appleby."

Jack was startled, and his heart beat a little quicker.

"Captain, I would wager my head, yes, my happiness, that you are mistaken about those girls. I have known them both all my life. While they are rather dashing girls and somewhat reckless in their speech and manner, there are not two better girls going."

"I would expect you to say that, Mr. Gordon, for you are very true to your friends."

"Let me see those letters—those Dollie Dux letters. Have you got them with you? Or have you abandoned the idea that the writer of them is the person you want?"

"No, to both questions. I haven't the letters with me. And I haven't abandoned that idea."

"But you recollect that Dollie Dux is a married· woman?"

"Well, you can't always tell," replied the Captain. "The person who wrote those 'Dux' letters is a very cunnin' person. She has played a big hand in this here affair, and hasn't left a trace—a footstep—behind her excepting those letters, and they are of the most guarded kind. The husband may be a stall for father or brother, or what not."

"I can't imagine either of those girls writing such letters," said Jack thoughtfully. "However, I am so certain you are on the wrong track, that I will engage to have specimens of their handwriting at my rooms, if you will come with the 'Dollie Dux' letters, before two o'clock to-morrow."

"All right, Mr. Gordon, I'll be there. And perhaps then I'll have something important to tell you."

"What is that?"

"I believe it's your rule, Mr. Gordon," said the detective slyly, "not to speak on suspicion ; you wait until you are sure."

"A very fair hit!" laughed Jack, and the Captain went away.

Jack went back to Lucy, who asked what Captain Lawton wanted.

"He's on the wrong track, and is inclined to implicate one or two of our friends," he replied. "However, he is greatly mistaken, I am certain. Have you got that letter signed 'Dollie Dux,' with you, Lucy?"

"Yes, it is in my room with my private papers."

"Would you mind letting me see it again?"

"I'll get it, of course," as she sprang up to go for it.

"And, Lucy," said Jack, "have you any letters from Mollie Lowell or Lou Appleby?"

"Yes. I have several."

"Bring one or two of those you may properly show me."

"I can show you all of them. There is nothing in them any one may not see."

She ran away to her room. Jack stood up before the grate with his hands behind him.

"I am afraid the Captain is grinding it down. He is evidently working in our field. I am afraid—I am afraid there is a frightful scandal brewing."

Lucy returned and her face was grave; indeed, she seemed terrified. Jack was alarmed by her appearance. He took the letters she handed him hurriedly. Opening the first he found it to be a letter from Miss Appleby, and laid it on the table. He searched for one written by Miss

Lowell and placed it beside the other. Then he opened the " Dollie Dux " letter.

He laughed outright.

" Why, Lucy, you frightened me with your long face. There is nothing in common between the fine, long, and elegant penmanship of this 'Dollie Dux' letter, and the rapid scrawl, all ways for Sunday, of Mollie's, and the huge, masculine strokes of Lou."

He looked up at her greatly relieved.

But the terrified expression had not left her face.

" For Heaven's sake ! " he cried in alarm, " what is the matter ? "

" I've recognized the writing of that letter," she said, faintly, laying her hand upon the one signed " Dollie Dux."

" Hush! Don't mention a name," said Jack, her horror communicated to him. " Are you certain ? Are you not mistaken ? "

" I can't be. See." She drew from her pocket another letter and placed it beside the one signed " Dollie Dux." There could be no failure to recognize the similarity. It required no expert to determine it. The same long, slim, peculiar penmanship, the same characteristics and tricks of the flourishes. There was absolutely no doubt.

Jack turned over to the signature. He gave a great start. He looked at Lucy, and she was looking appealingly to him.

" Oh, Jack, this is terrible! "

" It is horrible—horrible. Who would have dreamt it ? "

" Oh, Jack, dear, can't something be done to save her ? "

" By Heaven! something must be done. She must be saved."

Just then they heard Mrs. Van Huyn calling

Lucy, and had barely time to put the letters out of sight before she entered.

" I think you have billed and cooed enough for one day, and I've come to put an end to it. Why, what is the matter, you both look terrified ? "

" We have just sustained a severe shock over some news of a dear friend of ours," replied Jack:

" Indeed, I hope nothing serious ? "

" Yes, she is in great danger."

" A lady ? Can you help her ? If you can, do so, for dear friends are scarce in this world."

Lucy, her eyes wet with tears, went over and kissed her tenderly, saying :

" We have had a dear, dear friend in you."

" We will do what we can for her," said Jack. " Lucy, I think I will call on the Doctor. I hear he is not right well."

Notwithstanding the reports that Jack's peccadillos were at the bottom of the difference between Lucy and her adopted father, he let few days go by without calling upon the Doctor—almost daily, in fact.

" Ah, do, Jack, and if he is seriously ill let me know."

" But you are not going before dinner, Mr. Gordon ? "

" Oh, yes ! " he laughed. " If I take more meals in this house, I would better bring my clothes and domicile myself here entirely."

Lucy followed him out of the apartment, and he found opportunity to whisper to her :

" Not a word to Mrs. Van Huyn ! "

" No, indeed, not a word."

She went back again to chat with her hostess.

CHAPTER XXVI.

THE DOCTOR PHILOSOPHIZES ON WRONG-DOING.

WHEN Jack was shown into Dr. Sherman's room, he found the doctor lying upon the lounge quite unwell and unusually glad to see him. Apart from the real liking he had for the old gentleman, he hoped and argued from the fact that he was always received with warm cordiality, that the Doctor could be brought to a point where he would forgive Lucy her deception.

"I am very glad you have come to see me," said the Doctor. "I am very lonely. I have been practically alone all day."

"That ought not to be," replied Jack. "Had I known earlier you were ill, I should have been here before."

"Thank you, John," said the old gentleman simply.

Jack chatted away with him for a long time, but was conscious that the old gentleman did not give him close attention. He seemed to be busy with his own thoughts. Jack at length stopped talking ; the Doctor did not notice it. After a long interval of silence, the Doctor spoke :

"John, I think you are a better man than I am."

"Well, sir," said Jack laughing, "I rather think I'd have the best of you in a boxing or wrestling match. There is some difference in our ages and weights—in my favor."

The old gentleman laughed heartily at Jack's willful misapprehension.

"I don't mean that, John," he replied. "I think there is more charity in your soul than there is in mine. I think you look with a more kindly and generous eye upon the faults of others."

"If I do," answered Jack, "it must be because I have so many of my own, I want charity for my-self."

"I don't know about that either. I think you have a good heart—are naturally inclined to defend rather than attack people. And I think also you have that mental qualification which enables you to weigh exactly the wrong—its extent and degree."

Jack did not follow the old Doctor clearly, but he knew he was getting to a point of some importance.

"I have been examining myself since I have been lying here, John, and I am quite satisfied that one-half, if not fully three-quarters, of the indignation I felt against Lucy was not because she had committed a wrongful act, but because it had been committed against me. Now, as a matter of fact, what was wrong in her act was wrong because of it, not because it was committed against me. Yet that is not the way most people measure wrong. I am inclined to believe I do not. I think you do. It is astonishing how a wrong which you have regarded as a great one shrivels up when you view it from that standpoint."

It was undoubtedly very stupid of Jack not to realize the drift of the old man's philosophizing, but he didn't. He contented himself with saying :

"I presume that is so, sir."

The Doctor was silent again, apparently lost in thought, and Jack let him meditate. After a while the Doctor spoke :

"I've been thinking of another thing too. I have been thinking that, contrary to the usual teaching, it is much harder to repair by confession the consequences of wrong than it is to refrain from its original commission. There is the shame, the humiliation, the fear of the unknown consequences attending the confession, and the influence of one's environments, the fact that the next day is as good a day as the present one ; and so delay succeeds postponement, and postponement delay, each day the confession being made more and more difficult. Interests, affections, and what not, perhaps ambitions, all spring up to delay and restrain it."

The old man relapsed into silence again, and Jack sat watching him closely, speaking never a word to interrupt the current of his thoughts.

" Then how easy it is to commit a fault ! ' continued the Doctor. " People who have not been subjected to great temptation can not realize how circumstances will force a person into wrong-doing. Sometimes one is just trembling on the brink, the wrong word at the right moment urges them over, or the right word at the right moment restrains them. Do you ever read Hugo's 'Les Miserables,' John ? It's a great book. It preaches a great sermon. You remember how the circumstance of the starvation of his sister's children forced Jean Valjean into the crime of theft of bread for them ? In the goodness of his heart and full of divine pity he committed that theft. You remember, too, how after having gone down in the depths, crushed into darkness of soul by the tyranny of law, he is lifted up and light given him by that lie of the Bishop? Ah, John, there are some lies that are not wrong. They are blessed acts. One should be charitable, should be broad with the faults of the young. Instead of crushing them down with punishment, they should take them by the hand, lead them toward the light—forgiving. The spirit of forgiveness and of broad charity,—that is the beautiful thing about our Christ."

He was silent again, and Jack did not interrupt his silence.

"For instance, Lucy was undoubtedly sorely tempted. The situation in which she stood was a trying, nay a terrible, one for a young, unformed girl, whose mind had not had that training it would have had had she been possessed of a mother. Yet I doubt if she would have committed that wrong had it not been for the tempter who stood beside her to say the wrong word at the right moment. I was very fond of her, John."

He ceased talking again. And Jack did not reply. Presently the old gentleman struggled to a sitting posture and cried most irritably:

"Why don't you speak, John? I am sick. I am lonely. D— it, can't you see? I want Lucy."

"Yes, sir, I see. I've been waiting to hear you say so."

"Then why don't you bring her to me? What are you delaying for?"

"Yes, sir, she shall be here to-morrow morning," replied Jack, "early, if you will give me your word that you will make it easy for her to come to you; that you will not upbraid her with bitter words; but will receive her repentance with tenderness."

"Oh, John, I want her! I don't want to find any fault. I don't want to blame her. I want her tender, sweet face about me again. Go and bring her, John. Bring her early. Tell her that you bear my full forgiveness."

"Doctor, I never bore a message with greater gladness. The cup of my happiness is full to running over. We are to be married on the twenty-third, and I dearly hoped that this might occur before that event. After that we go to live in our own house, and in that house there is a corner for you."

He wrung the old man's hand and hastened away with the glad news to Lucy.

There were friends of the family at the house, whom Lucy was assisting Mrs. Van Huyn to entertain, and when Jack made his appearance with his beaming face, she knew something glad had occurred.

So entirely unlike himself was he in his want of repose and composure, that she finally said to him:

" Jack, you have some great news."

" Yes.   Great indeed for you.   And I know Mrs. Van Huyu will excuse you while I communicate it."

They went off together to the room Mrs. Van Huyn had assigned them, and there, to Lucy's great joy and satisfaction, she learned that she had become necessary to the Doctor and that he desired her return,—that he had asked it without being solicited.

" Now," said Jack, " I want you to write your sweetest note to the Doctor.   Write it in a penitent spirit, and I promise you you will never hear from any one again a word about Lucy's fault."

" Lucy's crime, Jack, for such it was," she said. " Yes, I'll do it."

" Where's the paper?" said Jack, getting up and searching over the table in the center of the room.

" There, in that old-fashioned secretary in the corner.   Lift up the cover and you will find it in a drawer."

" But which one?" said Jack; " there are a lot of them."

" The one which is not locked.   All the rest are locked but the paper drawer."

Jack pulled at one and the other, and in fumbling about touched the spring of a secret drawer, and it flew out.

" Heavens!" said Jack, as he caught a glimpse of its contents.

" What is it ? " asked Lucy.

" Nothing," he said with altered voice, as he closed it up quickly. " I have stumbled upon a private drawer, and got into things I ought not to have done. Ah, here's the paper."

He brought it to her, and they busied themselves with the composition of the letter which was to be the beginning of the reconciliation between Dr. Sherman and Lucy.

CHAPTER XXVII.

A BAFFLED DETECTIVE.

QUITE early in the morning following the events described in the last chapter, Jack accompanied Lucy from the residence of Mrs. Van Huyn to the B—— hotel, where Dr. Sherman anxiously awaited her. He walked with her as far as the door of their rooms and left her, discreetly refusing to be a witness of the reconciliation.

Hastening back to his own apartments, he barely had time to don his lounging jacket and draw a writing-table close to the grate fire, for the morning was cold, before Captain Lawton's card was presented.

"You are prompt, Captain," said Jack, after he had exchanged greetings with his visitor. "I have kept my word and have the letters."

"I have brought the 'Dollie Dux' letters," replied the detective, taking from an inner pocket the dainty little missives of the unknown "Dollie," folded the long way of the paper and confined by a small rubber band. He removed the elastic ring, laying the letters in front of Jack, and drew up a chair to the table.

"This is a matter quickly disposed of," said Jack. "It is, as I said, folly to endeavor to conneet those girls with this affair."

He took from the table the two letters Lucy had given him the night previous, and spread them before the detective.

Captain Lawton opened one of the " Dollie Dux " letters and placed it beside the two.

He smiled as he looked.

" No," he said, " it is plain. The writings are not the same. That lets them out."

" If you knew the young ladies you would know that neither of them could have written the letters if they had tried. But may I ask why you suspected them ? "

" I suppose," said the Captain slowly, " you would say upon insufficient basis. About two weeks before the murder, at a Saturday afternoon matinée, these two young ladies occupied a box at the theater where Renfrew was playing, and amused themselves and the company on the stage, so an actor told me, with wildly flirting with that fellow." Then, suddenly breaking off, he said : " You are mistaken about ladies of society not using pat-chouli—it seems to me they all do more or less. These two young ladies do occasionally."

He pushed the letters of Miss Lowell and Miss Appleby across the table to Jack, and laid the letter of " Dollie Dux " he held in his hand with its fellows. Jack was for the moment lost in thought and did not notice the act, nor that the detective took from his pocket a small wallet, from which he drew a narrow slip of paper.

" The murderer is now figured down to five," continued the detective, "and I'm betting that the name of the one I'm looking for is one of the three on that paper."

He laid it immediately in front of Jack, who picked it up mechanically and read the names.

He burst into laughter.

" Captain," he cried, " you select strangely for your suspicions. I think if you had every woman's name in New York to select from, you could not have chosen three less likely to be placed under suspicion. Within three weeks I have dined at the house of each of these ladies. I must have their letters somewhere."

He crossed the room to a desk standing between the windows, and tumbled the papers which littered it about in his search. The detective watched him slyly.

Presently he returned, bearing three letters with him.

"To be sure," he said, "the penmanship of these is more like that of ' Dollie Dux ' tnan Miss Appleby's or Miss Lowell's ; yet so different you need not be an expert to determine, at a glance, how absurd it is to attempt to find ' Dollie Dux ' among the writers of them."

The Captain examined them with great care. He laid them on the table, saying simply :

" And yet they all use patchouli."

"I fear, Captain," said Jack, laughing, "you are off the scent while following scent."

The detective grinned over the joke, but did not reply. He compared them again. With a sigh he pushed them aside.

" That disposes of three more," he said.

Jack started at this remark, and turned an inquiring look upon the detective.

Captain Lawton wrote deliberately two names on a blank piece of paper, and pushed the slip in front of Jack.

" Then it must be one of those two names," he said, eyeing Jack keenly.

Jack laid his hand upon the slip without looking at the names.

" Captain," he said, sternly but calmly, "you are a shrewd man—a very shrewd. man—you have laid a cunning trap for me, and I nearly put my foot in it. By this process of exhaustion you are making me your aid to detection. By reason of my anxiety to protect those from suspicion I knew could not be implicated, you have succeeded in getting me to eliminate one after another, until you have gotten down to two. Now, if it should appear on reading these names that again I saw one I was quite certain ought to be free from suspicion, you leave me in the position of having charged the other with being the person you want. It is a cunning game, but it must end right here. I won't go with you another step. You charged me some time ago with having treated you unfairly. I acknowledged the charge, and by my considerate treatment of you have tried to show regret for my bad manners. I think now you are open to the charge."

"I don't think so, Mr. Gordon," replied the detective ; "it is for you to choose whether or not you will express an opinion. It is in your own hands."

"Yes, but, Captain," persisted Jack, " your trap was laid all the same. You expected me to read the names and cry out that one, at least, did not do it. I can not help what the consequences may be, or who may get hurt, I shall have nothing more to say on the subject. Your trick is a sharp one, and nearly succeeded."

The Captain smiled his inscrutable smile again. Jack picked up the paper and read the names. He gave a start, which he quickly repressed, but not so quickly that the Captain did not observe it. He smiled again. Jack laid the slip of paper down ; his face bore a troubled expression.

"Well," said the detective.

"I have nothing to say," said Jack doggedly.

"You were surprised to see one name on that list ?"

"To see both of them."

"See here, Mr. Gordon, this has been a particularly hard case for me, and I have worked in the dark from the beginning. I need assistance, and I think I can give you good reasons why **you** ought to assist me."

Jack looked at him coldly.

"You see," said the detective, settling himself back in his chair and looking over Jack into the bright fire in the grate. "You see, you told me Renfrew's right name was Jacob Myers; that he was a cousin of Miss Sherman's; that she went to school at Rocky Point; and that these people came from about Cornwall."

He cast a glance at Jack, who was regarding him with a moody face.

"I made some inquiries," continued the detective, "up in that country, and found some people who knew Miss Sherman's parents and Myers as well. I learned something about Dr. Sherman's young days."

"Well," replied Jack irritably, "and what has all that to do with me?"

"I know what was in those letters Miss Sherman wrote to Renfrew, and why she didn't want Dr. Sherman to know."

He looked hard at Jack, who had thrust his hands deep in his pockets and was staring the table out of countenance. Receiving no reply the Captain went on, and, as Jack acknowledged, he had gathered the truth.

"Well?" he said aloud.

"I've no call to tell that story to Dr. Sherman, but if I don't you ought to consider I don't do so because of a friendly feeling to you. And that is a friendly act that ought to be repaid by you in assisting me."

"You're climbing the wrong tree, Captain," said Jack, rousing up. "You couldn't tell Dr. Sherman anything he doesn't know now,"

It was the Captain's turn to be surprised.

" How is that ? " he asked.

" After I found out what the secret was, which being possessed by Renfrew gave him power over Miss Sherman, I insisted that the Doctor should be told. It has been told him without reservation, and he has forgiven everything."

The Captain had played the last card in his hand, the one he had reserved for a great stroke, and to his manifest disappointment he found it was not a trump. His chance of success lay in obtaining Gordon's willing or unwilling assistance. He had tried to secure it by force, by persuasion, by trickery, and finally through an appeal to Gordon's selfish interests. He had failed in all. What course should he now pursue ? On the table lay a disorderly little pile of papers, notes and letters. Thinking deeply, lost to his surroundings for a moment, almost unconscious of his act, he stretched forth his hand and pulled out the sheet lying under all and placed it on the top of the pile ; he continued to take the under sheet and place it on the top mechanically, and thus bid fair in time to make every sheet the under one and top one in turn.

Jack watched him with a dissatisfied expression. He was by no means pleased to learn that the detective was in possession of Lucy's secret. He had believed it confined to Lucy, Dr. Sherman, and himself. Now a fourth knew it. Who would be the fifth ? And the sixth ? The prospect was not agreeable. He thought the detective was a meddlesome rascal who ought to be suppressed. He had trusted Lawton and had been betrayed. In short Jack was very angry with the detective and was meditating revenge.

While he was thus thinking and chafing, he watched the detective playing with the papers.

The Captain, still absorbed in thought, drew out a sheet on which something was written.

They both started at the same moment.

Each had recognized the penmanship.

The Captain leaped to his feet and carried the paper to the window, where there was better light.

Jack followed, thoroughly frightened, and looked over his shoulder.

It read :

"Monday, Oct. 16.

" DEAR MR. GORDON :—My husband desires me to write you to say he would be glad to have you to dinner on Thurs-dry, the 18th, to meet Mr. ———"

Here it ended, the sheet having been torn across the page.

The detective hastily turned the leaf, but the rest of the paper was blank. The signature evidently had been on the first page.

Jack breathed more freely.

" That is the same hand as the ' Dollie Dux ' letters," asserted the Captain. " Who wrote that letter ? "

" I don't know," said Jack steadily. " I've forgotten."

" That isn't likely," replied the detective sternly.

" You see I have so many invitations I can't be expected to remember all who write to me," replied Jack.

" Humph ! I must have the other part of that letter."

" I don't know how you will get it," replied Jack warmly.

" I do. I shall take it," said the Captain, turning quickly to go to the table.

Jack, divining his purpose, sprang to the table, reached it first, and faced the Captain.

" You will recollect," said Jack fiercely, " that these are my private papers."

"Stand aside and let me do my duty," demanded the detective.

"I'll have no interference with my affairs," answered Jack, very pale and very angry.

"I'll have no interference with me," was the Captain's reply. "Get out of my way."

Jack did not move. The Captain took him by the shoulders in an attempt to thrust him aside.

The unexpected happened. As is often the case with athletic men, the Captain underrated his antagonist.

He felt himself lifted and shot through the air. He fell in a corner, astonished.

He recovered himself quickly, however, but only in time to see Jack sweep the contents of the table into the grate, and the papers blaze up fiercely.

With an oath he made a rush toward the grate, intending to rescue what he could, but Jack met him and pinioned him by the arms so that he could not move.

As powerful a man as was the Captain, he was as putty in the hands of Jack, nerved to superhuman effort by intense anger. The detective was astounded at the strength of the younger man.

"I am a patient man," said Jack between his teeth, "but you must behave yourself here. These are my rooms and everything in them mine. And, by Heaven! if you touch anything here, you'll never touch anything again."

By this time the blaze caused by the burning papers had subsided. Nothing was left but a heap of black ashes.

Jack released the Captain.

Both men were angry. Jack was the more angry of the two. They stood glaring at each other.

"Who murdered Renfrew? You know," sternly, nay fiercely, demanded Captain Lawton.

"I don't. If I did I wouldn't tell you."

"I ought to put you under arrest."

"Don't try it. I am in no mood to be trifled with."

"Do you call it trifling to do one's duty?" asked the Captain, the first to regain possession of him-self. "This is a serious thing you have done to-day—you have willfully obstructed the course of justice and the law."

"Don't preach to me. I won't have it," cried Jack, still trembling with anger and thoroughly enraged. "Leave the room. Leave it before I do you harm."

"Yes I'll leave it, but you will hear from me shortly, and in a way you won't like," said the de-tective. "Give me those letters I brought here."

He went to the table. There was nothing what-ever upon it. The letters were gone.

"Where are those letters?" he cried, turning upon Jack in alarm, his anger blazing up again.

"Burned I expect," replied Jack, surprise at their loss doing more to calm him than anything else.

Captain Lawton looked hastily under the table and on the hearth. Jack assisted him. They were nowhere to be found. Jack felt an unholy joy over their loss, and this joy presently put him in entire possession of himself.

Becoming satisfied that they were indeed burned when Jack had hastily swept everything from the table into the fire, he turned to Jack so angry that the words fairly hissed as he uttered them.

"My fine young fellow, you will have to account for this in a place where your impudence won't do you any good."

"Poof!"

"I've seen higher heads than yours knocked under, and, by high Heaven! you'll have to answer for this."

"Put a bridle on that tongue of yours," answered Jack, angry again. "If you had not attempted to rob me of my papers your letters would be safe now. You've attempted to bulldoze me before and failed. Don't try a second time. You may fare worse. There's the door. Get out."

The detective saw the rising anger of the other, and though he was by no means a coward, his commonsense assured him nothing was to be gained by prolonging an angry discussion.

He went to the door, and paused to say :

"You've baffled me now. But I'll beat you in the end, Mr. John Gordon. Take care you are not made a party to this crime."

"Leave the room."

The detective passed out, deep disappointment in his heart.

It took Jack a long time to cool down, but when he was composed enough to realize just what he had done, he acknowledged that he had gone too far and that in all probability he had made trouble for himself.

As he paced up and down the room, trying to imagine what effect it would have upon him and whether it was likely to interfere with his marriage, which had been that day announced, he saw a piece of paper protruding from under the cover of his desk between the windows. He pulled it out.

It was the other half of the letter, the endeavor to obtain possession of which had caused the quarrel with Captain Lawton. The half Captain Lawton had found lay on the floor, where he had dropped it in the struggle.

Jack picked it up and threw them both deliberately in the fire.

"I won't be tempted now to placate the Captain. What a lucky thing it was I swept those 'Dollie Dux' letters into the fire! With the other thing

out of the way, detection is now well-nigh impo
sible.''

He threw himself in a chair, lost in thought f
a long time. He was interrupted by the entranc
of his man Crimmins. This aroused him, and h
jumped up, saying :

" Now to dress and go to Lucy before anythin
interferes.''

OBLIGATIONS OF FRIENDSHIP.

WHEN Jack was shown into the Sherman parlor, an hour after his warm interview with Captain Lawton, all traces of his own heat had disappeared. The Doctor and Lucy were conversing pleasantly, nothing apparent to indicate that a rupture between them had necessitated a reconciliation. Having talked agreeably with them for some time, Jack said :

" Lucy, I came to ask you to call with me upon Mrs. Van Huyn. I do not think we have made proper recognition of her kindness."

" If you think so," said the Doctor, who was one of the most punctilious of men, " you should do so without delay."

So Lucy, glad to have some moments alone with Jack, ran off to prepare herself for a walk.

On their way Jack told Lucy the story of his stormy passage with Captain Lawton, and expressed the fear that the consequences might be serious. It was true, he said, that he did not believe Captain Lawton to be a vindictive man, but his pride was evidently enlisted in the search for the murderer of Renfrew, and he feared the detective would not take kindly the accident which had deprived him of about the only clue he had. When they had parted the Captain was quite evidently very much angered, and what he might do under the influence of anger Jack could not even guess.

The story of her lover greatly alarmed Lucy,

and before Jack succeeded in allaying her fears they had reached the residence of Mrs. Van Huyn. The lady was engaged in the room she had allotted to the use of Lucy and Jack, when the former was under her roof, and she received them there.

Glad to see them again, she told Lucy she had felt quite lonely over her departure. When she was informed of the happy reconciliation with Lucy's adopted father, she congratulated both in warm terms on the prosperous turn affairs had taken.

Seizing the opportunity to make his recognition of her kindness, Jack said quite pointedly, indeed Lucy thought with unnecessary elaboration, that Mrs. Van Huyn had put him under such obligations, that the lady could at all times, under all circumstances, and at all hazards, command his loyal friendship.

Perceiving the embarrassment of Mrs. Van Huyn under Jack's fervent protestations, Lucy successfully turned the conversation into other channels. Jack, who was plainly laboring under much excitement, became abstracted, lost part of the conversation, which, when he was appealed to, had to be repeated to him, before he could understand what had been said to him. So singular was his manner that Lucy was quite ashamed of him, and Mrs. Van Huyn began to think he had been indulging freely during the day.

This had been going on for some time, when Jack arose and said :

" I hope, Mrs. Van Huyn, you will pardon the liberty I am about to take. Yesterday, when Lucy and I were searching for paper to write a note, I accidentally made a discovery which interested me greatly."

He went to the secretary, mention of which was made in a previous chapter, and lifting the cover which formed the desk, pressed the secret spring he had discovered and from the drawer, which flew open at his touch, took a case.

Mrs. Van Huyn's face flushed red, and she cried in tones of pained surprise :

" Mr. Gordon ! "

Lucy was aghast at his freedom.

But he continued, regardless of their displeasure :

" When I was a lad of twenty I traveled in Europe with Mr. and Mrs. Jamieson, and while there made a present to Mrs. Jamieson of a brace ôf pistols with singularly carved handles. They were in a case similar to this."

He opened it.

" The pair was exactly like this one. There is one missing here."

Was it only anger over Jack's rudeness and freedom, that made the color leave the face of Mrs. Van Huyn, and a wild fright come into her eyes ?

" I always supposed," continued Jack, " that these ivory sides to the handles were not the ones originally made for the pistols—they were placed on afterwards to increase the value and beauty. Mrs. Jamieson kept them several years, but about two years ago her husband loaned them to some-body, he had forgotten who. Perhaps it was you and you have neglected to return them. I wonder if my theory is correct ? "

Mrs. Van Huyn sat upright and rigid, her face the color of marble, and as hard, her eyes fixed on Jack, her hands tightly clasping the arms of her chair. She did not seem to breathe.

Jack took from his pocket a knife and loosened the screws which held the ivory sides in place.

" Yes," he said, " I am quite certain they were put on to increase their value."

The two pieces dropped into his hand.

" They are of little use and would be far better out of the way."

He threw them into the fire.

Mrs. Van Huyn made no effort to restrain him. Still rigid and motionless, she sat staring at Jack with wild, frightened eyes and white face.

Lucy was utterly bewildered. She had not as yet penetrated Jack's purpose.

"These pistols usually come apart into several pieces," he continued, as he unscrewed them, throwing part after part into the fire.

"The contents have gone into the fire, the case should follow."

He broke it into several pieces and threw them in as well. Lucy was entertaining doubts as to Jack's sanity. But there was neither motion nor word from Mrs. Van Huyn, only that wild, frightened stare.

"There is something else I want to speak of, Mrs. Van Huyn," resumed Jack. "Some time ago, in behalf of Lucy here, I obtained some letters she had written from a person now dead. When I placed them in her hands, she found among them a letter which did not properly belong to the package."

He took a letter from his pocket, and opening it showed it to Mrs. Van Huyn.·

"It is signed ' Dollie Dux,' you perceive."

She made no effort to take it ; she did not even look at it ; she did not take her eyes from Jack's face,—those wild, frightened eyes,—but still stared at him, her lips colorless as her cheeks, parched and slightly parted ; her breast heaving.

Lucy understood now, and going to her old schoolmate and friend, sat beside her, taking her hand in her own.

"This letter should go into the fire as well," said Jack, throwing it on the coals and watching it blaze up.

He turned again to·Mrs. Van Huyn.

"The detective found other letters signed 'Dollie Dux,' and has been trying by their means to trace the writer. But those letters were all burned to-day ; not one signed 'Dollie Dux' remains. I burned them all to-day,—all of them, every one.'

Was it a gleam of hope that altered for a fleeting instant the expression of those stony blue eyes ?

"Nothing now remains," continued Jack. "No proof exists. Everything is destroyed. Nothing can be traced. 'Dollie Dux' will now never be found, unless she reveals herself, and I don't believe she will be foolish enough to do that. It would be well for her, however, if she were to leave the country for a while. But three persons in all this world have any certainty as to her identity : Herself, and two others, and these two will suffer imprisonment rather than reveal it. She may go in security and contentment, for she will leave those two behind her to watch her interests."

The hand of Mrs. Van Huyn was cold and lifeless, and she did not seem to know that Lucy was holding and chafing it.

"You are not well, Mrs. Van Huyu," said Jack. "Your husband goes to Europe shortly, and though I know you are disinclined to go, yet I think you should. It would improve your health. You should stay as long as you could."

"Come, Lucy," he said, after a moment, "Mrs. Van Huyn is not well. Her social duties have been too much for her, doubtless. If we stay longer we will weary her. Come."

Lucy rose, and bending over her old schoolmate, for whose misery and misfortune she had profound pity, kissed her tenderly, the tears streaming down her face.

Mrs. Van Huyu made no response, nor motion, that indicated she was aware of the caress. She still sat upright and rigid, her face white as marble, her wild, frightened eyes still on Jack, as if she were fascinated by him.

Jack and Lucy went out together, passing along the hall. They turned to look at her through the open door. She was kneeling on the floor, her arms on the table, her head buried in them. Her frame was convulsed with a storm of sobs ; tears had come to her relief.

"She is saved," whispered Jack, and they silently went into the street.

CHAPTER XXIX.

MARRIAGE BELLS.

ON the twenty-third of February, 1884, two events occurred. The Servia steamed out of the harbor at a late hour in the afternoon, bearing, among its passengers, Mr. and Mrs. Van Huyn for a lengthened stay abroad.

And—a matter of great importance to two of our friends—Miss Lucy Sherman was given away at the altar of Grace Church by Dr. Sherman, to Mr. John Gordon. The Bishop of the diocese solemnized the gift at twelve o'clock noon.

The reception after the ceremony took place in the ample parlors of Mrs. Jamieson, and the dainty little hostess fluttered like a humming-bird among the guests, so happy was she over the good fortune of her favorite. In this she vied with Dr. Sherman, who beamed on all with smiles and good nature.

The newly married pair stood under a floral bell of huge proportions, which " Dizzy " had insisted on providing and would not be denied.

To them came their friends to say pleasant words. Among them a lady and gentleman in traveling costume, apologizing that their trunks were already on the steamer, and saying they could not deny themselves the pleasure of wishing them well and happy for all their lives. The lady did a strange thing when she was unobserved. She took the hand of the groom, pressing a warm kiss upon

it, and after bending upon him a look of love
and gratitude hastened away.

Mollie Lowell and Will Robb came and passed
by with light and gracious words, but not until
Mollie had whispered to the groom :

" It's catching, Jack. I've been and gone and
done it too. Yes, to Will. He's advertising it by
his conscious looks."

" Dizzy " came with an eye on the bell to see
that it was plumb, and said :

" Jack, old man, you look so happy and your
bride so sweet, I almost feel like taking a stable
mate myself."

All whose acquaintance we have made in these
pages came, but the surprise of the day was to see
Captain Lawton struggling forward in the throng.
He had seized the opportunity to go on duty at
the house, that he might say pleasant words.

" I congratulate you," he said to Jack, slowly as
was his wont. " I congratulate you, Mr. Gordon.
You ought to be a happy man, and I suppose you
are. I've dropped that case ; it goes on the list of
undiscovered mysterious ones."

" Indeed ? " replied Jack. " How is that ? "

" I could not track it. The clues and proof
were all destroyed—destroyed accidentally. What
you can't prove it's no use to look after. Besides,
I guess the bird is flown—flown to Europe. It
ain't so bad. I'd like to have had the triumph.
But it don't harm me to have a miss once in a long
time. 1 can stand it."

Turning to the bride he said :

" I wish you joy, madam—joy all your life and
plenty of it. You have got a man to cherish and be
proud of. He is a man who takes more chances—
has taken more chances—for a friend than any man
I ever knew, or ever expected to know. And if he
will take them for a friend, what won't he do for the

wife he loves? He's a big, strong-hearted man, madam. But you're worthy of him, madam. And the worst wish I've got for myself is, that if ever I get into trouble, I shall have two such friends as you at my back. I wish you both joy."

He moved off to give room to others to offer kind wishes, but none were more sincere, though they may have been offered in more graceful phrase.

With the sound of the wedding bells still falling pleasantly on our ears, the pen is cast aside—the story is done.

THE END.

CPSIA information can be obtained
at www.ICGtesting.com
Printed in the USA
BVHW070906061218
534935BV00024B/566/P